Mistrust; or, Blanche and Osbright

Matthew Gregory Lewis

Mistrust, or Blanche and Osbright

A Feudal Romance

by

Matthew Gregory Lewis

CHAPTER I

—"The bird is dead.
That we have made so much on! I had rather
Have skipped from sixteen years of age to sixty.
To have turned my leaping time into a crutch.
Than have seen this!"
CYMBELINE.

Peace was concluded, and the waters of the Rhine again flowed through plains unpolluted with blood. The Palatine 1 saw his enemies at his feet; it rested in his own pleasure to trample or to raise them, and the use which he made of the victory proved how well he merited to be victorious. His valor had subdued his enemies; his clemency converted those enemies into friends. The Duke of Saxony,2 the hereditary foe of his family, had been made his prisoner in the last engagement; he restored him to liberty without ransom or conditions; and he could have framed none so binding as those, which this fearless generosity imposed on the Duke's gratitude.

Henry of Saxony became from that moment his firmest ally; and the Palatine found in his powerful friendship more real strength than if he had surrounded his whole dominions with a triple wall of brass.

The Saxons departed to their own country; the Palatine dismissed his feudatory troops; and their chiefs led back their vassals, loaded with the presents of their liege-lord, and proud of the wounds which they had received in his service. Among these warriors few had displayed more valor than the youthful Osbright of Frankheim; but no sooner was the war concluded than none panted with more impatience for the permission to depart. It was given, and the next hour saw him spring upon his courser; he committed the care of his vassals to a gray-headed knight, in whose prudence he could confide; and then, while his heart swelled high with joy and expectation, he gave his horse the spur, and sped toward his native towers.

But it was not the recollection of those native towers, nor of any one whom his castle-walls contained, which now made his cheeks glow and his eyes blaze with such impatient fire. It was not to embrace his beloved and loving mother; nor to kneel at the feet of his respected father, who held his two sons precious as the two apples of his eyes; nor yet to behold once more his little darling, the young Joscelyn, who looked upon his elder brother as the masterpiece of creation; none of these was the motive, which now hurried Osbright onward: none of these, while the mountains, woods, and wilds were left behind him with inconceivable rapidity, made him wonder at the unaccustomed sluggishness of his courser. No! It was the hope of once more 1 A ruler (count) of the Palatinate, one of two districts in Southwest Germany.

2 Henry the Lion, Duke of Saxony (in Northwest Germany) and Bavaria, died in 1195...beholding the avowed enemy of himself and of his whole house, that being to whom he was an object of the wildest alarm, and by whom his very name was held in abhorrence; this was the hope, which made the young warrior's heart swell with eagerness almost to bursting.

There was not a fleeter steed in the whole Palatinate than Osbright's; his speed was stretched to the utmost, but in vain. Night was at hand, and he had not yet arrived at the wished-for goal. The knight abandoned the fruitless attempt to reach it, checked his courser, and stopped for a few moments to gaze upon the hostile towers of Orrenberg, as they rose proudly in the distance, all golden and glittering with the splendors of the setting sun.

"Oh! yes!" he sighed to himself, "the day must at length arrive when I need no longer gaze at distance on yonder walls, and envy every pilgrim who dares approach the portals with the prayer of hospitality! The day shall surely come when my name, now never mentioned but with curses, or at least with alarm within the precincts of yonder castle, shall call down blessings only inferior to those given to its lord's; when the sound of my courser's tramp on the drawbridge shall seem to the hearer sweet as the merry bells which announce a victory; and when to proclaim that Osbright of

Frankheim draws near shall be to announce a holiday throughout Orrenberg. Till then, peace dwell in all your hearts, my beloved enemies! With every bead that he tells, with every orison that he breathes, Osbright of Frankheim shall call down blessings on the heads of those, who now call down curses on his!"

Again he set forward, but now suffered his horse to choose what pace he pleased. The wearied animal gladly profited by the permission. Osbright, plunged in melancholy but not unpleasing thought, observed not the moderate rate, at which he was now performing his journey; till the moon, emerging from behind a cloud, suddenly poured her radiance full upon his sight, and the unexpected light startled him from his reverie. He looked up, and saw the place before him, to reach which had been the object of his proceeding with such unwearied expedition. But it was already night, and the spell, which had drawn him thither so forcibly, had ceased to operate.

Still, though he knew well that the search must be fruitless, he could not refuse himself the satisfaction of revisiting that place, whose remembrance was so dear to his imagination, so consecrated by his heart. He bound his steed to the branch of a shattered oak, and entered a narrow path, which wound among the mountains. He soon reached an open space, nearly square in its form, surrounded on three sides with flowering shrubs and branches, and presenting on the fourth the entrance to a grotto, whose mouth was thickly overgrown with ivy, woodbines, and a variety of tangling weeds. Osbright heard the well-known murmur of the waterfall; his heart beat quicker as he listened to the sound, and his eyes sparkled in the moonbeams with tears of melancholy pleasure.

He entered the cavern; as he expected and feared, it was vacant; but the moonshine, penetrating through an opening in the rocky roof, and converting the cataract into a flood of silver light, enabled him to see a wreath of flowers still fresh, which was lying on a stone seat at no great distance from the water. With an exclamation of joy he seized the wreath, and pressed it to his lips. The cave then had been visited that very day! Alt! if he had but reached it before sunset...

But the sun was not set forever; tomorrow it would rise again, and he now doubted no longer that it would rise a sun of joy to him. He kissed off the dew-drops, with which the flowers were heavy, and which he could not help flattering himself were tears of sorrow for his absence. He then hung the garland round his neck, and having deposited his well-known scarf in place of the flowers, he quitted the cavern with a lightened heart, and with hopes increased by the certainty that in his absence he had not been forsaken..And now this first and chief anxiety dispelled, he was at liberty to bestow his thoughts on those friends who were the next dearest objects of his affection, and on that home where his unexpected arrival was certain to diffuse such joy. Again he spurred his horse forward; but the animal needed no inducement to make him exert all his speed, while retracing a road whose goal was so well known to him. He darted forward with the rapidity of an arrow and would not have paused till his arrival at the castle of Frankheim had not Osbright checked him when within half a mile of his paternal towers. The sound of a bell tolling heavily attracted his attention and gave his imagination the alarm; from the quarter whence it sounded, he guessed that it must proceed from St. John's chapel, a building raised by the piety of one of his ancestors long deceased, and whose vaults were appropriated to the sole purpose of receiving the reliques of those who expired within the walls of Frankheim. Vespers must have long been past; it was not yet midnight; nor indeed was it usual to celebrate religious rites within that chapel except on particular festivals or occasions of extraordinary solemnity. His heart beat high, while he paused to listen. The bell continued to toll, so slow, so solemn, as to permit his doubting no longer that it was sounding for the departure of some enfranchised spirit. Was there a death then in his family? Had he to lament the loss of a relation, of a friend, of a parent? Anxiety to have this question answered without delay, would not permit him to pursue his destined course. Hastily he turned the bridle of his horse and darted into the grove of cypress, whose intervening shades hid the chapel from his observation.

It was situated in the bosom of this grove, and a few minutes were sufficient to bring him to the place whence the sound proceeded. But the bell had already ceased to toll, and in its place, after a momentary silence, a strain of solemn choral music and the full swell of the organ burst upon the ear of Osbright. He knew well those sad melodious sounds: it was the "De Profundis" chanted by the nuns and monks of the two neighboring monasteries, St. Hildegarde and St. John.

The chapel was brilliantly illuminated; the painted windows poured a flood of light upon the surrounding trees and stained their leaves with a thousand glowing colors; it was evident that a burial was performing and that the deceased must be a person of no mean consideration.

Osbright sprang from his horse, and without allowing himself time to secure the animal from escape, he rushed into the chapel, while anxiety almost deprived him of the powers of respiration.

The chapel was crowded; and as he had lowered the visor of his casque,3 no one was disposed to make way for him; but within a few paces of the principal entrance there was a low door conducting to a gallery, the access to which was prohibited to all, except the members of the noble family of Frankheim. Too impatient to ask questions, which he dreaded to hear answered, Osbright without a moment's delay hastened toward the private door. It was not without difficulty that he forced his way to it; but all present were too much engaged by the mournful business which they had come thither to witness to permit their attending to his motions, and he reached the gallery unquestioned and unobserved.

Alas! It was empty! With every moment the conviction acquired new force that the funeral bell had knelled for some one of his family. His whole frame shook with alarm as he cast his eyes upon the aisle beneath. It was hung with black throughout; but the blaze of innumerable torches dispelled the double gloom of night and of the sable hangings. The sweet sad requiem still rose from the choir, where the nuns of St. Hildegarde were stationed. The avenues to the aisle were thronged with the vassals of Frankheim; but the middle of the aisles was left free, for there stood the chief actors in this mournful ceremony, and the crowd kept a respectful distance. By the side 3 Helmet..of an open grave, which occupied the center of the aisle, stood the Abbot of St. John's, the venerable Sylvester. His arms were extended over the grave, as if bestowing on the already consecrated earth an additional benediction. An awe-inspiring air of sanctity pervaded his tall thin figure; his eyes seemed to shine with a mild celestial brightness when he raised them with all the rapture of enthusiasm toward Heaven; but their fires were quenched by tears of pity when he cast a glance of benevolence toward a stately tomb of white marble which rose upon his left hand. Against that tomb (which was raised in honor of Ladislaus the first Count of Frankheim, and which was exactly opposite to Osbright's retreat) reclined the two chief mourners: a warrior and a lady; and the youth's heart felt itself relieved from a weight almost intolerable, when he recognized the beloved authors of his being.

Now then he no longer trembled for the life of one of those parents, whose undeviating affection through the whole course of his existence had made them so justly dear to him. But for whom then were they mourning? The loss must needs touch Osbright nearly, which could occasion such extreme affliction to his parents; and that their affliction was extreme, it was not permitted him to cherish even a doubt. The noble Magdalena stood with her hands clasped, her eyes raised to Heaven, while unconscious tears coursed each other down her cheeks; motionless as a statue; pale as the marble tomb, against which she was leaning; the very image of unutterable despair.

Widely different was the expression produced by anguish upon the noble and strongly-marked features of Count Rudiger. His heart was the seat of agony; a thousand scorpions seemed every moment to pierce it with their poisonous stings; but not one tear forced itself into his blood-shot eyeballs; not the slightest convulsion of his gigantic limbs betrayed the silent tortures of his bosom. A gloom settled and profound reigned upon his dark and high-arched eyebrows. He bent his gaze immutably upon a bier, which stood between himself and Magdalena, and which supported a coffin richly adorned with the escutcheons of the house of Frankheim. He rested one hand on the coffin; his other hand grasped firmly the jeweled handle of his dagger. His glaring eyes were stretched widely, as if their strings were on the point of breaking, and the flames which blazed in them were red and lurid. Disdain seemed to curl his lips and expand his nostrils; an expression of restrained fury pervaded his whole deportment; and his resolute attitude, and something almost like a sullen smile which marked itself round his mouth, gave the prophetic assurance of revenge dreadfully satisfied. His long sable mantle was wrapped round his right arm; it had fallen from his left shoulder, and hung round him in loose drapery; while its folds rustled wildly in the night wind, in whose blast the tapers were flaring, and whose murmurs seemed to sigh for the deceased, when the nuns pausing in their mournful melody permitted its hollow voice to be heard. With every fresh gust the white plumes, which decorated the four corners of the bier, waved themselves backward and forward with a melancholy motion; and then did the tears stream faster from Magdalena's eyes to think that now nothing of motion remained to the being whom she had ever loved so fondly, except the waving plumes with which his hearse was decorated.

And now the moment was come for depositing the coffin in the earth. The music ceased; a profound and awful silence reigned in the chapel, only interrupted by the loud sobbing of a young page, who had thrown himself on his knees and who, by enveloping his head in his cloak, had endeavored without success to prevent his grief from becoming audible. Though his face was thus concealed, his light and graceful form, the long tresses of his dark golden hair which streamed in the night wind, and still more the enthusiastic extravagance of his sorrow, left Osbright no doubt who was the mourner. It was the young Eugene, Count Rudiger's beloved but unacknowledged offspring.

Four of the friars had now approached the bier; they raised the coffin in silence and bore it toward the open grave. The heavy sound of their departing footsteps roused Magdalena; she extended her arms toward the coffin and started forward a few paces, as if she wished to detain the bearers. But a moment's recollection was sufficient to make her feel the inutility of delay; and folding her arms across upon her bosom, she bowed her head in humble resignation. Her lord still remained without motion.

The coffin was lowered gently into the grave; it disappeared, and the attendants were on the point of covering it with the appointed marble, when Eugene uttered a loud shriek.

"Oh! Not yet! Not yet!" he cried, while he started from the ground, and rushing forward, he arrested the arm of one of the friars, who held the monumental stone. His eyes were swollen with weeping, his gestures were wild as a maniac's, and his voice was the very accent of despair.—-"Oh! not yet!" he exclaimed. "He was the only being in the world that ever really loved me! The slightest drop of blood in his veins was dearer to me than those which warm my own heart! I cannot endure to part with him for ever! Oh! not yet, father! good father, not yet!"

The youth was now kneeling on the verge of the grave, and he bent down his head and bathed the friar's feet with his tears in all the humility of supplication. As yet Magdalena had borne her sorrow like a heroine; but the unexpected shriek of Eugene, the heart-piercing hopeless tone in which he pronounced the words of "for ever!" was more than her fortitude could bear. She uttered a deep sigh, and sank insensible into the arms of her attendants; while Rudiger (whom the page's cry of agony had also roused from his gloomy meditations) sprang forward with a furious look, and plunged into the grave.

With involuntary horror the friars started back, and then as if changed to stone by a Gorgon's head, they remained gazing upon the dreadful countenance, which presented itself before them.

Count Rudiger's stature was colossal; the grave in which he stood, scarcely rose above his knees.

His eyes blazed; his mouth foamed; his coal-black hair stood erect, in which he twisted his hands, and tearing out whole handsful by the roots, he strewed them on the coffin, which stood beside his feet.

"Right! right!" he cried, while his thundering voice shook the vaults above him, and while he stamped upon the hallowed earth with impotent fury. "Right, Eugene! Not yet shall the earth cover the innocent victim of avarice! Not yet shall the lips of holiness pronounce the last long farewell! Not till I have sworn upon his coffin never to know rest, till his death is avenged most amply; not till I have devoted to the demons of darkness the murderer and his accursed offspring!"

"Yes, yes! Not he alone, but his whole serpent-brood shall pay the penalty of his crime, his wife, his children, his servants, all! all! His vassals shall be hunted through the woods like wolves, slaughtered wherever found; his towers shall be wrapped by my hand in flames, and its shrieking inmates hurled back into the burning ruins! You hear me, friends! You see the agony which tortures my heart, and yet do I curse alone? And yet does no voice join mine in the vow of revenge?—Nay then, look here!—Observe this pallid face! Observe this mangled bosom! Look on these, look on these, and join with me in one dreadful irrevocable curse."

"Vengeance! Everlasting vengeance on the bloody house of Orrenberg."

As he said this, he violently forced open the coffin, tore from the shroud a lifeless body, and held it up to the gaze of the shuddering multitude around him. It was the corpse of a child apparently not more than nine years old; a large wound disfigured the ivory bosom; yet even in death the countenance was that of a sleeping angel. His eyes were closed; as Rudiger held it forth at his arm's length, the profusion of its light flaxen hair fell over the pale lovely features of the child; but Osbright had already seen enough to confirm his worst suspicions. His brain whirled round, his sight grew dim, and he sank lifeless upon a bench which stood behind him. Yet as his eyes dosed, and before his senses quite forsook him, he could hear the exasperated multitude answer his father's demand by a general shout of—"Vengeance! Everlasting vengeance on the bloody house of Orrenberg."

CHAPTER II

—-"Suspicion's lurking frown and prying eye."—
R. P. Knight's, "Landscape."

The visor of Osbright's helmet was closed, and the exclusion of air necessarily prolonged his insensibility. When he recovered himself, the chapel was vacant, and the lamps and torches all extinguished. The total darkness, which surrounded him, added to the confusion of his ideas; and a considerable time elapsed, before he could recollect himself sufficiently to arrange in their proper order the dreadful circumstances which had just occurred. The image of his murdered brother haunted his imagination, and resisted all his efforts to chase it away. Though his own education had been received principally at the court of the Bishop of Eamberg, and therefore he had seen but little of the young Joscelyn, that little was sufficient to make him feel an affection most truly fraternal for the amiable child. Deeply therefore did he regret his loss; but yet he regretted the circumstances which attended it even more than the loss itself. His father's horrible curse still rang in his ears; the sentence of death pronounced upon himself would have sounded to him less dreadful, than that general shout of the incensed vassals— "Vengeance on the house of Orrenberg!"

Bewildered, irresolute, daring scarcely to admit the possibility of his father's solemn assertion being unfounded, and heaving many a sigh of anguish over the probable ruin of all has schemes of happiness, did Osbright quit the gallery and pursue his way to the great entrance of the chapel.

The darkness was profound, and he reached the gates with some difficulty; but here he found his intention of departure completely frustrated. During his swoon the doors had been carefully locked and barred, and though his strength was great, it was still insufficient to enable him to force them open.

Exhausted with his fruitless efforts, he abandoned the attempt, and had made up his mind to return to the matted gallery and remain there quietly till morning should enable him to regain his liberty; when he recollected, that at the further extremity of the aisle there existed a cell, which generally was tenanted by one of the Brethren of St. John, whose office it was to keep the chapel in order, and by whose care in all probability the doors had been so carefully secured. Thither he bent his way, hoping to obtain his freedom by the friar's assistance, and at least certain of finding a less damp and unwholesome shelter for the night.

Feeling his way from pillar to pillar he proceeded slowly and cautiously. It was not long, before a ray of light at some distance guided his steps, and a low murmuring voice assured him that the cell was inhabited. He pushed the door gently open. A lamp, which was placed in the nook of a narrow Gothic window, threw its light full upon the pale face and gray locks of the friar, who was kneeling before a crucifix, with an immense rosary in his hand, and his eyes fixed devoutly upon the Redeemer's countenance. Osbright was both too unwell and too impatient to wait for the conclusion of his prayer; he stepped into the cell, and the sound of his heavy spurs, which clattered as he trod, roused the monk from his devotions. He started up and looked round, amazed at so unusual an intrusion. But no sooner did he cast his eye upon his visitor than he fell prostrate upon the earth before him, loaded him with benedictions, and poured forth a profusion of thanks to Heaven, which had thought the meanest of its servants worthy of so unusual and distinguished an honor. Osbright had raised his visor for the benefit of air; and the singular beauty of his features, the noble expression of his countenance, the symmetry of his form, and the dazzling brilliance of his armor, made the pious brother conclude that he was honored by a celestial vision, and that the form who stood before him was no other than the Archangel Michael. He was so convinced of this that he was on the very point of asking news of the Dragon when the knight hastened to dissipate his illusion.4 "Rise, good father!" said he; "I am a mortal like yourself, and what is more, am a mortal who greatly needs your assistance. During the late mournful ceremony, a sudden illness overpowered me. I became insensible; no one observed me, and I found myself on my recovery alone, in darkness, and inclosed within the chapel. Doubtless, you possess the means of opening the gate, and can restore me to liberty."

"Truly can I, my son," answered the monk; "and it is but just that I should be the person to let you out, as I was the person who locked you in so carefully. Mercy on me, poor old man! I little thought, that I was locking in anything better than the dead, and myself, and my old raven Jojo."

"But oh! all ye blessed spirits! You must have been ill indeed, sir knight; for the poor child that Count Rudiger tore out of its shroud did not look paler than you do at this moment. Nay, in truth, it was your paleness, which made me be so sure of your being a spirit when I first looked on you; for I thought, that no living thing could have had a countenance so bloodless. But how I stand here talking when I ought to be doing somewhat to assist you!—Here, sir knight!" he continued, at the same time hastening to a small walnut-tree cupboard, and spreading his whole store of provisions before the stranger; "here is some refreshment—here is bread—and fruit—and hard eggs—and here is even some venison for you; for alas, the day! I am old and weak, and our Abbot has forbidden my fasting and keeping the spare holy diet, which I used, and which I ought to keep. Alt! I shall never have the good fortune to be a saint, nor even a martyr, Heaven help me! But I will not murmur at Providence, sinner that I am for saying so! Now, good sir knight, eat, and refresh yourself, for it makes my heart bleed to see you look so pale. And see! I protest, I had like to have forgotten the best of all. Here is a small bottle of a most rare cordial; it was given me by Sister Radigonda, the fat portress of St. Hildegarde's, and she assured me that its virtue was sovereign. Now taste it, good son, I beseech you! I am sure it will do you service; not that I ever tried its good qualities myself; but Sister Radigonda has, and she's a devouted person, who (I warrant you) knows what's good. Now taste it, dear sir knight! In the name of St. Ursula and the eleven thousand virgins 5 (rest their souls, though nobody was ever lucky enough to find their blessed bodies!) I beseech you, now, taste it!"

The benevolent manner of the old man was irresistible. Osbright partook of the cordial, and the warmth which immediately diffused itself through his chilled veins, and the glow which it produced upon his cheeks, sufficiently testified that Sister Radigonda had not said too much in favor of her present. Brother Peter now pressed the youth to partake of the viands placed before him; and Osbright, finding that his person was totally unknown to the monk, thought that by engaging him in conversation he might most easily and expeditiously learn the meaning of the 4 St. Michael, prince of angels, was commonly depicted in art as a dragon-slayer.

5 A legendary Cornish princess, supposedly slain by the Huns along with the 11,000 virgins that she was escorting in eleven galleys to France..melancholy transactions, which he had just witnessed in the chapel. Accordingly, he took some of the refreshments, which his host presented to him, and found no difficulty in leading the conversation to the funeral and its cause; while on the other hand Father Peter, believing his discourse to be directed to a stranger, whom curiosity alone had led to the chapel, and who had no personal interest in the transaction, felt no hesitation in answering the questions put to him without disguise and in their fullest extent.

"You shall hear all that I know, sir knight," said the old man; "and I believe, I know more of the matter than most people Indeed, you'll marvel perhaps, how I came to know so much; but did you remark a young page at the funeral who sobbed so piteously that one heard him in spite of the organ? His name is Eugene; he is the Countess's page, and (between ourselves) they do say that he is more nearly related to the Count, than law and religion allow of; but the Count wishes this to be kept a secret, and so I shall not say a syllable upon the subject. Well! this Eugene is an excellent pious youth, and often comes to the chapel, and prays upon his knees for whole hours together before the Virgin's image, and employs all the money he can procure in purchasing masses in hopes of removing the soul of his poor sinful mother out of purgatory—and so he used often to bring the poor little murdered Joscelyn to visit me in my cell, and he told me the whole matter exactly, as I now tell it you. You must know, sir knight, that some twenty years ago, there was an old

Count of Frankheim, by name Jeronymus, who bequeathed his large domains..."

"Nay, pry'thee, my good Father," interrupted Osbright impatiently, "proceed to the murder at once, and leave out the bequest of Count Jeronymus!"

"Leave out the bequest?" cried Brother Peter. "Heaven help us! you might as well bid me tell the story of the Fall of Man, and leave out the Apple! Why, that bequest has made the whole mischief; and into the bargain, sir knight, I must tell my own story my own way, or I shall never be able to tell it at all.—Well! as I was saying, this Count Jeronymus had but one child, a daughter; and as his ruling passion was family pride (of which, however, the present Count has a hogshead, where the old one had but a drop), he resolved to bestow her hand and his large domains upon the next heir. Unluckily, before his intentions were made known to him, the next heir was already affianced to another. Rudiger of West Frankheim and his cousin Gustavus of Orrenberg, equally needy and equally related to Jeronymus (only Rudiger was the eldest branch) were both suitors to Magdalena, the rich heiress of Helmstadt, who at this very moment chose to make her election in favor of the former. Now who was puzzled but the old Count? What should he do? Family pride forbade his alienating the patrimony of Frankheim from the man who at his death would be the reigning Count; and yet paternal affection would not suffer him to leave his unoffending daughter quite destitute. To reconcile these two jarring passions, he bequeathed the whole hereditary estates to Count Rudiger, and gave his daughter the Lady Ulrica his whole personal property, besides several purchased estates of considerable value, together with permission to bestow them and her hand according to her own free choice. That choice fell on Gustavus of Orrenberg, who was too greedy of wealth to refuse so advantageous a match; though he never forgave the Lady Magdalena's rejection of him; but cherished a secret spite in his heart against her and his successful rival."

"Indeed? Is that quite certain?"

"Oh! quite, quite! Why, Count Rudiger always said so himself! Though to be sure Gustavus carried himself artfully enough toward him, and would fain have been on friendly terms at Frankheim. But Rudiger was too prudent to be deceived, and guessed that all these fair speeches and mild looks were intended to lull him into a dangerous security, till an opportunity should offer of doing him an injury without danger."

"And did Gustavus ever betray any such intention by his actions?"

"Oh! Blessed Virgin! No, to be sure not! My lord was too much on his guard to give him an opportunity! It's true, the families still kept up an appearance of being on decent terms, and even visited; but my lord never went to the castle of Orrenberg but well armed and attended, and kept an eye of suspicion on everything that was passing around him; and when Gustavus returned the visit, he must easily have seen by my lord's looks and manner that he was aware of his being come for no good; and so he never ventured to put his evil designs in execution.—But how my old head rambles! I forget to tell you that there was a worse cause of enmity than their joint-suit to Magdalena! You must know that when Count Jeronymus found his daughter's choice to have fallen upon Gustavus (who, after Rudiger, would inherit the titles of Frankheim), he bethought himself of a way to render the union of that beloved name and his large possessions more durable than ever. Accordingly in a clause to his will he enacted, that in case either Gustavus or Rudiger should die without heirs, the property, which he had bequeathed to the one, should descend to the other undiminished. Neither of them had children at the time of the old Count's decease; but within a twelvemonth after it, Rudiger fell dangerously ill. He lay for two days insensible; the physicians believed him to be dead. The report spread over the whole country; and oh! in what haste was Gustavus to take possession of the castle and its domains! He came galloping over in all joy, when lo and behold! he found our good lord still in the land of the living, and was obliged to return home quite chapfallen! If the plague had broken out among them, it could not have produced more sorrow in the castle of Orrenberg than the tidings of this recovery!"

"Indeed! Who told you that, Father?"

"Oh! I remember that it was the common report throughout Frankheim; I never heard anyone say otherwise. Well! sir knight, Gustavus had scarcely got the better of this disappointment when he met with another. The Lady Magdalena proved with child, and was safely delivered of a fine boy, who was christened Osbright. When Gustavus heard this, he turned as white as a corpse!"

"How know you that? Did you see him?"

"I? St. Chrysostom 6 forbid! I never saw the hypocritical assassin (Heaven pardon me for calling him so, who am myself so hardened a sinner!). I say, I never saw him in my whole life, not I! I would as soon look on Beelzebub in person! No, no! I might indeed have seen him once; but I cast down my eyes, crossed myself, and passed on. Well, the house of Orrenberg comforted itself with thinking that Rudiger had but one son, while the Lady Ulrica had borne four, besides a daughter. It's true, Count Rudiger's prudence had made him send the young Osbright out of the reach of their enmity; but still he might be taken off by a thousand natural accidents. This hope also received its death-blow about nine years ago by the birth of a second son to Rudiger, this very little luckless Joscelyn. The two boys increased in bloom and strength, as they increased in years; while the Orrenberg children were all weak sickly creatures. One after another, the three eldest sank into the grave; but when about six months ago the fourth boy expired and left them with only a daughter and without hopes of further progeny, Gustavus's spite and avarice could no longer contain itself within bounds. He resolved to remove the objects of his aversion, cost what it might; and you saw in the mangled body of Joscelyn the effects of this diabolical resolution! Heaven pardon him and me, and all sinners, Amen!"

6 St. John Chrysostom (345-407), Greek churchman, Bishop of Constantinople..

"Aye, that murder, Father! That murder... that is what I would fain hear! Oh! Proceed, proceed, for pity's sake! Let me know every cruel circumstance... even though to hear it should break my heart!"

"Ah! and that would be a thousand pities, for it must needs be a kind heart to take on so grievously at hearing a story in which you have no concern.—Well then! You must know, that one morning the Count set forth to hunt the hart, and his young son pleaded so earnestly to accompany him, that the father could not resist his entreaties. The sport was excellent; and in the eagerness of pursuit everyone forgot to look after Joscelyn. At length the animal was taken; the hunters found themselves at a considerable distance from home; by degrees they all assembled, all except Joscelyn. Now then a hue and cry commenced; the Count was half frantic with apprehensions, and his alarm was increased tenfold, when he discovered that the chase had beguiled them into the woods of Orrenberg. Away rode the hunters, some one way, some another; four of the most trusty followed Rudiger, and while he made the forests ring again with the name of Joscelyn, the hand of Providence, in order that the murderer might be punished, guided him to the place where the poor child had already breathed his last; it was near a small river; the ground was stained with blood, and a huge wound stood gaping upon his ivory bosom."

"Search was made for the assassin, who (it was evident) could not have gone far, for the body was not yet cold! And a man, whose garments were still crimsoned with blood, and whose countenance pronounced him capable of committing any mischief, was found concealed in a thicket at no great distance."

"And what reason had he for..."

"Oh! sir knight, every one guessed at the reason as soon as Martin (the Count's squire) exclaimed that he knew the assassin, and that he was one of the Count of Orrenberg's domestics."

"The villain too knew in whose presence he was, and addressing Count Rudiger by his name, he fell on his knees, and entreated him not to hurt him; a sure proof of his being conscious of some crime, else why should he have been apprehensive of receiving hurt, sir knight? Well! He could not deny his belonging to Gustavus, but for a long time he persisted in swearing that he had found the child already insensible in the wood, and that the blood had stained his clothes while èonveying him to the rivulet, in hopes that by bathing his face with water he might restore him to his senses. Truly, the fellow was artful enough, and made out a good plausible story; but Rudiger was not easily to be deceived. He had the villain conveyed to the castle of Frankheim, and there proper means were taken for extorting from him a confession of the truth."

"And what was that confession?"

"Exactly what everyone expected; that he had been commanded to murder the child by his master, Gustavus of Orrenberg."

"He confessed it?—Almighty powers! Are you sure, that he confessed it?"

"Sure of it? Why, alas-the-day! I heard him say it with my own ears. He was asked by the Count who set him on to commit the murder, and I heard him answer as plain as I now hear you—'Gustavus of Orrenberg.' "

"Is it possible!" exclaimed Osbright in agony. His last lingering hope was now destroyed, and with all his anxiety to believe Gustavus innocent, he found himself unable to exclude the irresistible conviction of his guilt.

"Ah! It is but too certain!" resumed the friar with a deep sigh. "One would willingly disbelieve the existence of such villainy, but I heard the assassin own it myself; and a hardened sinner he was! In spite of all my pious exhortations to repentance, not a word would he confess, though I begged him with tears in my eyes; for wicked as he was, it almost broke my heart to see the tortures which he endured, and all out of his own obstinacy! Since the very moment that he made the desired confession, my lord ordered him to be taken from the rack, though it was then but to little purpose."

"The rack?" exclaimed Osbright, seizing the old man's hand with a convulsive grasp. "Was it then only on the rack, that he made this confession?"

"No truly; till Count Rudiger had recourse to torture, not a syllable would he utter, but assertions of his own and his master's innocence. Nay, even when he was actually on the rack, he persisted in his obstinate falsehood. He had already remained there so long that he was scarcely unbound, before he breathed his last, poor sinful wretch! Heaven pardon him and take him to its mercy!"

Now then the heart of Osbright again beat freely. It is true, the death of his brother made that heart the abode of deep sorrow; but to banish from it the belief that Gustavus was the boy's assassin was to relieve it from a burden of insupportable agony. That belief grew weaker with every question which he put to Brother Peter; he found that while in possession of his strength and faculties the supposed culprit had most strenuously denied all knowledge of the crime; that the excess of torture alone had forced from him the declaration that Gustavus of Orrenberg had any concern in it; that the name of Gustavus had been suggested by the prejudices of the suspicious and already exasperated father; and that the whole confession was comprised in the mere pronouncing that name when the speaker was seduced into uttering it by the certainty of immediate release from tortures the most excruciating. Osbright had been educated at a distance from his family, and his mind therefore had not imbibed the prejudices which made the Count of Orrenberg be considered as an incarnate fiend throughout the domains of Frankheim. His liberal nature inclined him to wish all hearts to be as pure and benevolent as his own; and his judgment was both too candid and too keen to mistake assertions for proofs or to be deluded by the artful coloring in which prejudice ever paints the actions of a detested object. In defiance therefore of all his father's endeavors, he had resolved to suspend his opinion of Gustavus, even while his character was a matter of indifference to him; but now that the dearest of all interests made him wish to find him worthy, to have found him so deeply culpable would have wrung with excess of torture the most susceptible fibers of his heart.

On reflection, he found that his plans must be delayed till the innocence of Gustavus in this bloody business could be fully cleared to the satisfaction of Count Rudiger and of all Germany; and he silently vowed never to know rest till he had proved that innocence, and ascertained, beyond the power of doubting, the real name of the monster whose dagger had sent the blooming Joscelyn to an untimely grave.

But how was he to commence his inquiries? Brother Peter was so fully convinced of the guilt of Gustavus that his answers to Osbright's questions only served to mislead his search, instead of furnishing the unraveling clue to this mystery of iniquity. The youth anxiously desired to talk over the business with some unprejudiced person; and for this purpose he resolved to depart immediately for the castle of Sir Lennard of Kleeborn. This worthy knight was, in spite of their alienation, considered equally as a friend by the two families of Frankheim and Orrenberg; Osbright had seen enough of his character, during his last visit at his father's, to feel for him the highest sentiments of esteem and reverence; and he resolved to lay his difficulties, his hopes, and his fears before this excellent man without disguise, and entreat his assistance in forwarding the one and removing the others.

The moon shone bright; in defiance of the friar's entreaties he resolved not to wait for morning, since grief and anxiety would have prevented sleep from visiting his couch. However, being anxious to avoid the presence of Count Rudiger till the first emotions of grief for the loss of his child, and of passion against the house of Orrenberg, should have subsided, he requested the monk to allow him to find hospitality within his cell on the succeeding night, when (as he said) his affairs would necessitate his being again in the chapel's neighborhood. His request being readily granted, he charged the old man to conceal his visit from everyone; and then having enforced his charge, by a considerable present to be appropriated to the use of Brother Peter's patron saint, Osbright vaulted upon his courser, whom fidelity had detained near the chapel, and whose frequent neighing had already announced his impatience at the absence of his lord.

CHAPTER III

"Alas! the spring-time's pleasant hours returning
Serve but to waken me to sharper pain.
Recalling scenes of agony and mourning.
Of baffled hopes, and prayers preferred in vain!
Thus was the sun his vernal beams displaying.
Thus did the woods in early foliage wave.
While dire disease on all I loved was preying.
And flowers seemed rising, but to strew his grave."
Charlotte Smith.

While the castle of Frankheim resounded with cries of agony and threats of vengeance, the spirit of tranquil sorrow reigned on every brow and in every heart throughout the domains of Orrenberg. Seven months had elapsed since the death of the heir of those domains, the young and amiable Philip; the wound was skinned over, but the pain was still felt; tears had ceased to trickle, but the heart had not yet ceased to bleed.

Gustavus stood at an oriel-window, and contemplated the fertile fields, which he hoped on his deathbed to have bequeathed to his darling. The Lady Ulrica was employed at her tapestry-frame; but her work was often suspended, while she cast a look of anxious tenderness on the lovely Blanche (who was at work beside her), and while she breathed a mental prayer that Heaven in mercy to an almost broken heart would preserve to her this, her loveliest, her dearest, her only remaining child.

The silence was interrupted by the entrance of an old female domestic, who informed Blanche that she had at length found the canvas bag which had been so long missing, and which she now presented to her. Blanche hastily quitted the tapestry-frame, while her cheek alternately colored with anger, and grew pale with apprehension.

"Oh! Rachel!" she exclaimed in a tone of reproach, "how thoughtless to bring it hither! alt! and see! My dear mother has recognized it but too surely, for her eyes are already filled with tears!"—And she threw her arms affectionately round the waist of Ulrica, and entreated her pardon for being the occasion of suggesting such painful recollections.

"What is the matter?" demanded her father, advancing from the window. "What distresses you, Ulrica?" Then glancing his eye on the canvas bag, which Blanche had suffered to fall upon the ground, "Ah!" he continued, "I need no answer! Those are the playthings of my poor dead boy! What would you do with them, Blanche?"

"I meant to give them to the gardener's children; they were Philip's playfellows and friends, and they have not forgotten yet, how dearly he loved them. It was only yesterday that as I passed toward St. Hildegarde's grotto, I met the poor children going to adorn Philip's grave with their choicest flowers; and their father tells me, that they mention him every night in their prayers, and never pass a day without visiting his monument—and so I fancied that by giving these playthings... But I wish that I had never thought at all about them, since the sight of them has distressed you so much, dear mother! Nay now, pry'thee, weep no more! You know, my father says that 'tis sinful to murmur at the dispensations of Providence, and that it gives him pain whenever he sees our tears!"

"And should not that reflection check your own, my Blanche?" inquired Gustavus. "Why are your cheeks so wet? Fie! fie, my child!"

"Alt! Dear father, I cannot prevent their flowing, do all that I can! When anyone seems happy, I cannot help smiling; and when anyone dies, surely I needs must weep. But at least I obey you better than my mother; indeed neither of us talk of Philip, but then she always thinks of him and is always melancholy. Now I am always gay, and endeavor not to think of him; except when something brings him suddenly before me, and then I cannot choose but weep, or else my heart would break in two;—for instance, when I look at these playthings, it seems to me as if Philip were present. I think I see him

24

arranging his troops so busily on the ground; I think I hear him entreating me to leave my tiresome tapestry and observe how bravely he will fight the battle."

"'The blue,' he used to say, 'are the vassals of—Orrenberg, and the red are the vassals of Frankheim; and now..."

"Of Frankheim, Blanche?" interrupted Gustavus, "no, no; that was not what Philip called them. 'The red,' he used to say, 'are our enemies.' "

"Yes, yes; our enemies, the vassals of Frankheim."

"You misunderstood him, Blanche; why should Philip call the vassals of Frankheim our enemies?"

"Nay, dear father, are they not so? Everyone in the castle thinks and says it."

"They, who say so, had better not say it in my hearing. The Count of Frankheim is my nearest relation, a man of singular military prowess and distinguished by many noble qualities. It is true, the dissimilarity of our manners and habits, together with various other impediments, has prevented so cordial an intimacy between the families as should exist between such near connections; but still I entertain a high respect for the character of the owners of Frankheim, and shall not hear without displeasure those persons called my enemies, whom I would willingly boast of as my friends."

"Your friends? Oh! Father! Would you call those your friends who have poisoned your only remaining son, who have deprived me of an only remaining brother? Ah! Should I not call these cruel people our enemies, our worst of enemies?"

"Poisoned my son? Poisoned Philip?"

"Nay, it is the common talk of the whole castle! Every child on the domains knows it, as well as I do, and trembles at the name of

Rudiger, the ruthless child-murderer! Nay; has not my mother openly acknowledged that..."

"Blanche!" interrupted Ulrica hastily, "you go too far. You misrepresent the fact. What have I ever openly acknowledged? I merely, in confidential conversation, let fall a hint, a sort of suspicion... that it was just possible... that to judge from appearances... that I was almost tempted to imagine..."

"Aye, Ulrica," replied her husband, "I feared from the very first that you were the original cause of this ill-founded report. Is there no hope then that my entreaties and advice will ever eradicate from your mind the only dark speck which deforms it? Of all the defects of the human heart, there is none more encroaching, more insidious, more dangerous than mistrust; viewed through her distorted optics, there is no action so innocent, no everyday occurrence so insignificant, that does not assume the appearance of offense. Words are misconstrued; looks are interpreted! Thoughts are guessed at and acted upon, as if thoughts were facts; the supposed fault is retaliated by a real one; that one gives birth to more; injury succeeds injury, and crime treads upon the heels of crime, till the web of mischief and misery is complete; and the suspector starts in surprise and horror to find both himself and his adversary equally involved in that guilt which but for his suspicions would probably have been the lot of neither."

"Nay, Gustavus, why thus severe? What have I done? I assert nothing; I accuse no one. I merely hinted at the possibility... and that, while I have life and conscience, I must maintain—-to die so suddenly! today in all the bloom of health, and tomorrow in his coffin! Oh! That fatal inheritance! To that shall I ever ascribe the loss of my child!—And then the livid spots, which broke out upon my poor boy's corpse... and the agonies which he suffered... the burning heat, and the insatiable thirst which tormented him... and above all the rapid putrefaction... Yes! yes! the moment that I beheld that, I exclaimed—'such a death cannot be natural.' A dreadful light broke in upon me, and..."

"—And at that light you have kindled a torch, capable of burning to the very ground the house of your unsuspecting neighbor, of your nearest relation! You have inflamed the imaginations of the giddy unthinking multitude, whose rage if once let loose and countenanced by their superiors..."

"I inflamed them? Oh! You injure me, my husband! It is true, their rage, their hatred against the Count of Frankheim is at this moment extreme; but I have done my utmost to prevent their breaking out into violence. I dread Count Rudiger; but I hate him not, for I will not hate any one; and though your former love for Magdalena once made me fear her influence over your heart, your uniform kindness during many long years has totally erased all such apprehensions from my bosom. Do not then suspect me of stirring up our people to vengeance upon the Frankheimers."

"Alas! It needed no instigation of mine to make them understand a tale so clear, a fact so evident that the murder circulated from lip to lip, ere I had time to impose silence on the deathbed attendants; and every man's own consciousness suggested to him the murderer's name."

"A tale so dear, Ulrica? Before your father's fatal bequest had raised suspicions of each other between the families, you attended Magdalena's lying-in—the child lived but a few hours, and expired in your arms. Had Magdalena been as mistrustful as yourself, how well would the tale have been told that, jealous of my former attachment to the mother, you had privately, while pretending to kiss it, confined the windpipe of the child, or pressed its skull together, or else. . ."

"Oh! spare me, my husband! Yes, such a tale might have been told... Oh! horror! might perhaps have been believed. I will say nothing more; I will accuse no one in future; I will bury all my suspicions in oblivion; I will forgive all... if they will but leave me this one blessing, this one darling, this my last, my only existing child!"

As she said this, Ulrica threw her arms round her kneeling daughter; and she was still weeping upon her neck; when a domestic entered, and announced a herald from the castle of Frankheim.

As all intimacy between the families had ceased, and they now only met on great festivals, or at tournaments, or on some solemn occasion, it was concluded that the herald's business related to some public occurrence, some imperial edict, or some regulations for the welfare of the Palatinate. The women, therefore, thought proper to withdraw. Ulrica, greatly agitated by the conversation which had just taken place, retired to indulge the agony of maternal regret in her own solitary apartment; and Blanche...? The war was concluded; the troops were dismissed; the knights were returning home.

"Perhaps!" said Blanche, and with a light step and heart full of hope, she fled through the secret passage toward the cave among the rocks.

CHAPTER IV

—"Oh! my soul come not thou into their counsels; unto their assembly. mine honor, be not thou united; for in their anger they slew a man, and in their self-will they digged a wall. Cursed be their anger, for it was fierce, and their wrath, for it was cruel." —GENESIS.

And the hopes of Blanche were not quite disappointed. It is true, the cave was vacant: but he had been there; but he had left a token that she was not forgotten by him. Tomorrow according to their mutual agreement she might depend upon seeing once more the youth whose image gratitude had engraved upon her heart in characters never to be effaced; and then might she claim his promise of revealing to her his real name and clearing up the mystery in which he had hitherto enveloped all that related to him, except his adoration of herself. Satisfied of that most material point, she had hitherto been content to leave every other in obscurity; but now she should know everything; now her lover would disclose himself, and authorize her disclosing their attachment to her parents; and precious as they held her, she still feared not their opposing her union with a man whom she loved so tenderly and by whom she was so tenderly beloved.

Besides, her father was sinking into the vale of years; the family required some younger and more active champion to defend them against the nefarious designs of their mortal foe, the cruel and insidious Count of Frankheim; and where could they find a fitter protector than this unknown knight who had already proved the strength of his arm and valor of his heart so successfully when he rescued her from the banditti? Oh! When once his bride, she should no longer tremble at the dreadful name of Rudiger! All then would be peace, security, and happiness! And while she made these reflections, she pressed the well-known scarf to her lips a thousand and a thousand times.

The sun was setting, and it was time for her to return home. She threw herself on her knees before the crucifix which she had herself placed on the rough-hewn altar; she poured forth a prayer of fervent gratitude to St. Hildegarde, traced a cross upon her forehead and bosom with the same holy water which had formerly quenched the thirst of that virgin martyr, and then bidding a tender adieu to the cavern in which she had passed so many happy moments, she sped back toward the castle, the scarf fluttering in the evening breeze as she retraced the secret passages.

She was proceeding toward her own apartment, when in crossing a gallery which was connected with the great hall, she was alarmed at seeing several of the domestics hurrying backward and forward in confusion; she stopped, and listened; she heard her father's name frequently repeated, and at length caught some words, as if some accident had happened to him.

Now then everything else was forgotten in the apprehension of his being in danger. She flew toward his apartment, which was on the other side of the castle; but in crossing the great hall, she was detained by the young Baron of Hartfeld..."Heaven be thanked, that I have found you, lady!" said he, taking her hand affectionately. "The Countess charged me to seek you, and prevent your being suddenly alarmed. Nay, look not so terrified! On my knightly word there is no danger, and a few hours will restore your father to that fortitude, of which the too great sensibility of his nature has at present deprived him."

"Oh! what has happened? What has overcome his fortitude? Something dreadful surely! Is he ill, Sir Ottokar? Oh! Assure me at least, that he is not ill!"

"His illness is merely temporary; by this time no doubt it is quite past. It is true, his senses forsook him for a time; he fainted, and..."

"He fainted? Oh! Heavens! Let me hasten to him this moment..."

"You must not, till you are more calm. Your present agitation would affect him and probably occasion a relapse. Suffer me to lead you into a less public apartment; there you shall hear all that has happened, and when your spirits are composed, you shall then carry peace and consolation to the wounded feelings of your father."

But the emotions of Blanche could admit of no delay; she still hurried onward; and as in fact Sir Ottokar had only wished to detain her, in order that he might enjoy her society for a few minutes without restraint, all that he had to communicate was told, before they reached the Count's chamber-door.

Interlarding his discourse with many compliments to his auditress and insinuations of the tender interest which he felt for her, the Baron now related that the business of the Count of Frankheim's herald was to accuse Gustavus of the assassination of the Count's youngest—son, and to proclaim open and inveterate feuds between the families of Frankheim and Orrenberg.

This the herald had not only announced to Gustavus in the most disrespectful manner, but had thought proper to repeat the purport of his mission publicly in the courtyard; at the same time accompanying his speech with such insulting remarks upon their master and his whole family, that the indignation of the vassals became outrageous, and threatened the insolent herald with consequences the most dangerous. The Count of Orrenberg was alarmed at the tumult and hastened to the courtyard to appease his incensed people, whose affection for them was unbounded. Gustavus was but lately recovered from a perilous malady, occasioned by grief for the loss of his last male heir; he was still in a state of lamentable weakness, and the shock of being so unexpectedly accused of assassination had greatly increased the irritability of his nerves, which naturally was excessive; yet still he exerted himself most strenuously in endeavoring to quell the confusion. But in vain did he command his vassals to be silent and temperate; in vain did he conjure the herald to be gone, if he valued his own safety. The insolent emissary persisted in heaping taunt upon taunt, and slander upon slander. The people grew more incensed with every word that he uttered; and at length overcome with agitation, heat, fatigue, and weakness, Gustavus sank into the arms of his attendants, and was conveyed to his apartment in a state of insensibility. However, he was already nearly recovered when Ulrica requested Sir Ottokar to seek her daughter and relate what had happened, lest she should be unnecessarily alarmed.

But Blanche loved her father too dearly to believe that he was quite out of danger till her own eyes had convinced her of his health and safety. She found him very pale and feeble, and his recollection was yet scarcely clear enough to permit his perfectly understanding the events which had taken place. Blanche sank on her knees by the couch, on which he was reposing, and threw her white arms round his neck affectionately.

"You have heard it all, my child?" said Gustavus. "You know, of how dreadful a crime your father is accused? But surely you will not believe me capable of..."

"Nor she nor anyone can believe it," interrupted Ulrica, "except those who are interested in working the destruction of you and all your house. Nay more; everyone, except yourself, knew well, that sooner or later the rancor and avarice of Count Rudiger must end in open war; but I little thought that he would have advanced so gross a falsehood as an excuse for commencing hostilities! They to accuse you of murdering a child! They, who themselves but seven months ago deprived us..."

"Peace! Peace! Ulrica; no more of that! —But tell me... my ideas are still so wandering...Is it then true, that Rudiger's son is murdered?"

"It is but too certain. He was found dead in one of our forests, and what makes the fact mor'e distressing is that one of our domestics was the assassin. He confessed his crime on the rack, and died in a few minutes afterward; died (horrible to tell!) with a lie still warm upon his lips. For oh! my husband, in his last moments he declared that he had been bribed by you to assassinate the poor child!"

"By me?" exclaimed Gustavus, and started from his couch. "Confessed it? No, this is not to be endured! Under such an imputation there is no living. Bring my armor; saddle my steed! I will hasten this moment to Frankheim; I will assert my innocence with all the irresistible energy of truth; I will demand to be tried by every ordeal, by fire, by water... Nay, nay, detain me not, I must to Rudiger this instant, and either convince him that I am guiltless, or perish by his hand."

He was rushing toward the door, but all present hastened to impede his passage.

"Count, this is insanity!" exclaimed Sir Ottokar. "You are rushing on inevitable destruction! Rudiger is not to be convinced. He has vowed your destruction with the most solemn and terrible adjurations; nor your destruction only; his vengeance includes all who are related to you, all who love you! Your wife, your daughter, your very domestics..."

"My daughter?" repeated Gustavus, clasping his hands in an agony of horror, "my innocent Blanche?"

"All! All are involved in Count Rudiger's plan of vengeance! He has sworn to give your castle a prey to the flames, and to feed them with its wretched inmates. No man, no woman, no child, no, not the very dog that now licks your hand, shall be suffered to escape! This did I myself hear the Count of Frankheim swear last night at the burial of his murdered child; and his friends, his servants, his vassals, all made St. John's vaults echo, while with one voice they repeated the bloody, the diabolical oath. My friendship for you, my lord, and my alarm for the safety of the Lady Blanche, made me hasten homeward to summon the assistance of my followers; they are mounted to the number of forty, well-armed and accoutered, and I have conducted them hither prepared to spill the last drop of their blood in vindication of your innocence, and in defense of the Countess and your lovely daughter."

"I thank you, Sir Ottokar, and should there be no means of avoiding this unnatural war, I shall profit with gratitude by your kind and ready friendship. But still I indulge the hopes of peace. I have no real fault toward Rudiger; and could I but contrive a personal interview with him...could I but explain the injustice of his suspicions... at least I will make the attempt; and perhaps... Ha! well remembered! Kurt," he continued, addressing himself to a gray-headed domestic, who was standing near the door, "is the herald yet gone?"

"Gone?" repeated the old man, shaking his head with a smile of satisfaction. "No, truly, nor likely to go, the villain!"

"Then call him hither instantly. He shall bear my request for an interview with Rudiger, and...How is this, Kurt? Why do you still linger here? I would have the herald come to me; bring him this moment!"

"Bring him? Why, aye, to be sure I could easily do that; but as to his coming, he'd find that a difficult matter... unless he can walk without his head. Nay, my lord, it is even so, and now all's out—the people's rage was not to be bridled; when they saw you fall, they thought that the herald had stabbed you; they fell upon him, men, women, and children, like so many mad people, and before one could say 'Aye' his head was off his shoulders, and nailed over the gateway between the two great kites."

"Ulrica! Ottokar!" stammered the Count, and seemed, as if he had been struck by a thunderbolt. "Is this true? Has my castle indeed been polluted by so horrible an outrage?—-Almighty powers! the murder of a herald... a character, ever held sacred even among the most barbarous nations... murdered in my own castle... almost in my own sight. Now then indeed the mischief is irremediable. From the imputation of this guilt never shall I be able to clear myself in Rudiger's eyes!"

"Nay, my dear lord," replied Sir Ottokar, "let not this misfortune affect you so deeply. The insolent menial merited well such a fate; a fate which (I can witness, as I arrived in the heat of the tumult) you did your utmost to avert. But to save him was not within the power of a mortal.

"His calumnies... his threats against your whole family... Your people's hatred of Rudiger. . .their consciousness, that he had deprived you of your son Philip by poison..."

"Aye, aye!" exclaimed Gustavus, "hear you that, Ulrica? Now then you see the fatal effects of your mistrust! Now then you enjoy the bloody fruits of those ungrounded suspicions, which you so lightly infused into the minds of the rash and wanton multitude! Oh! my wife, I fear greatly, that at the day of judgment when this murder is cited, your hands will not appear quite bloodless! God forgive you!"

The Countess shuddered, but only answered by a flood of tears.

"Spare your lady, my noble friend," said Ottokar, taking the Count's hand. "Even if your reproaches are deserved, they now come too late, and the present difficulties demand our attention too much to admit of reflections on the past. The Frankheimers are powerful and inveterate. Rudiger has sworn the extirpation of your whole family; Osbright is returned from the wars to assist his father's plans of vengeance; these human wolves thirst for your blood, and...earth and heavens! can it be possible? It is... it must be the same! Pardon me, Lady Blanche; by what strange accident do I see that scarf in your possession?"

"This scarf? You know it, sir knight?—I came by it... that is... I found it...as I was passing through the secret passages, which lead..."

"The secret passages? Osbright of Frankheim lurking in the secret passages of Orrenberg Castle?"

"Osbright?" exclaimed Ulrica in the greatest alarm. "And—you traversed those passages alone?—Oh! my child, from what a danger have you escaped! No doubt, his purpose there..."

"Must needs have been hostile to the inmates of this castle!" interrupted Ottokar eagerly.

"Perhaps... perhaps, he was aware that the lovely Blanche frequented those secret passages and hoped that his dagger might unobserved revenge..."

"Oh! no, sir knight," exclaimed the affrighted Blanche, "you misunderstood me! No one was lurking in the secret paths! It was not there that I found the scarf, it was in the cavern of St. Hildegarde... and perhaps you mistake about the scarf, too! Perhaps, it is not Osbright's! Oh! no, no, no! Heavenly mercy forbid that it should be!"

"Indeed?" said Ottokar, while jealousy whispered a thousand suspicions to his mind, "nay, of that there is no doubt. It is the work of the Lady Magdalena, and too remarkable to be mistaken."

"Besides, in saving the Palatine's life in battle, Osbright's bosom was slightly wounded; his scarf was stained with blood, and I heard him swear that the blood shed in his sovereign's defense was the noblest ornament of his scarf, and should never be effaced—look, lady, look! Osbright has kept his oath."

Blanche looked on the bloody marks; the scarf fell from her hands, and she clasped them in an agony of despair. With every moment did Sir Ottokar's jealous fears grow more strong, and his desire to impress Blanche with an idea of Osbright's animosity more keen and anxious.

"But one thing more!" said Blanche with difficulty, while she almost gasped for breath—"that horrible curse, which you spoke of... which Rudiger... which his vassals pronounced...was it pronounced by Osbright? Was Osbright in the chapel, when it was pronounced?"

"He was, lady! He was!" replied Ottokar, eagerly and peremptorily. "I was near the chapel door, and saw him rush into the chapel with a maniac's look, his eyes burning with vengeance, his lips pale with passion, his whole frame trembling with eagerness, and with fear lest he should be too late to join in the horrible execration. I heard Count Rudiger devote to destruction your father, your mother, your innocent self! I saw Osbright rush furiously forward to join his father; and instantly every voice except my own re-echoed the dreadful words—'vengeance! everlasting vengeance on the bloody house of Orrenberg!'"

"And did not one kind voice," said Blanche faintly, "did no suggestion of pity...ah! did no one utter one word to plead for the poor Blanche?"

"No one, lady! No one, as I have a soul to save!"

"Oh! I am very faint, my mother!" murmured Blanche, and bursting into tears she sank upon the bosom of Ulrica.

Her pale looks and trembling frame greatly alarmed her parents; but believing her agitation to be solely produced by apprehension and by horror at the dreadful threats pronounced against her life by the Frankheimers, they advised her to retire to rest and compose herself. Blanche willingly accepted the permission of departing, and hastened to meditate in the solitude of her chamber on the fatal discovery, which accident had just made.

CHAPTER V

"Let no one say, that there is need
Of time for love to grow;
Oh! no; the love, which kills indeed.
Dispatches at a blow.
"Love all at once should from the earth
Start up full-grown and tall;
If not an Adam at his birth.
He is no love at all."
Lord Holland from Lope de Vega.

While these transactions were passing at Orrenberg, Osbright was anxiously employed in finding means to remove all existing prejudices, and establish a close and lasting amity between the rival kinsmen. He found Sir Lennard of Kleeborn willing to assist his design, and scrupled not to lay before him the dearest secret of his bosom.

So great had been his father's apprehensions of treachery on the part of Orrenberg, that Osbright was seldom suffered to visit his paternal mansion. Year after year, however, having passed away without any fatal effects arising from the supposed avaricious views of Gustavus, and the youth being now of an age to take his own part, Count Rudiger about nine months before had gratified himself and his fondly anxious consort by the recall of his first-born son. The breaking out of hostilities compelled Osbright to leave the Castle of Frankheim a second time; but previous to his departure it had been his fortune to rescue the lovely Blanche from the hands of ruffians, and at the same moment to receive and impart a passion the most ardent and irradicable.

Blanche declared her name to her deliverer and earnestly entreated him to accompany her to the castle of Orrenberg, where her parents would receive their child's deliverer with all the warmth of heartfelt gratitude; but Osbright's prudence forbade his taking so dangerous a step, especially when the discourse of his mistress convinced him how deeply engraved, and how odious in their nature, were the prejudices attached to the name of Frankheim in the minds of the inmates of Orrenberg. Educated himself at the court of Bamberg, his heart was untainted by the gloomy mistrust which (with the solitary exception of Magdalena) he found prevailing throughout his father's domains; and the knowledge of Blanche's family name instantly suggested to his fancy the pleasing hope that their union might be the means of extinguishing the animosity which prevailed between two families so nearly related; but he found that the mind of Blanche was very differently modeled. The Lady Ulrica was naturally of a temper timid and suspicious. Jealousy of her lord's early attachment to Magdalena had originally disposed her to consider the actions of the Frankheimers in no favorable point of view; her father's unfortunate bequest made her regard them as persons whose interest must necessarily lead them to wish for the extinction of her family; a variety of trifling circumstances, which her jaundiced imagination made her see in false colors, strengthened her in this persuasion; and the successive deaths of four sons thoroughly persuaded her that she had not evil wishes alone to fear on the part of those who would benefit so greatly by depriving her of her children. All these ideas had been imbibed by her only remaining offspring. Blanche from her infancy had been accustomed to pray, that the Virgin would preserve her from Satan and the Frankheimers; at the mention of Rudiger's name she never failed to cross herself; and while she was thanking Osbright for her rescue from the ruffians, he could scarcely help smiling at the positiveness, with which she assured him of their having been emissaries either of his wicked father or of his bloodthirsty self!

Till these prejudices so deeply-rooted could be effaced, Osbright thought it absolutely necessary to conceal his name and to refuse Blanche's invitation to visit the castle of Orrenberg.

At the drawbridge he respectfully took his leave, and in return for his service, he only requested her word of honor, that she would not mention her adventure to any human being. Though surprised at the entreaty, Blanche could not refuse to give this promise; not to mention that she was herself apprehensive that if the danger which she had run should be made public, her mother's anxious care would never again suffer her to pass the walls of Orrenberg. This promise therefore she gave readily; but she hesitated a little when the unknown youth expressed an ardent hope that he should in future be permitted to thank the Lady Blanche for her compliance. To permit such interviews unknown to her parents, and when even herself was ignorant of his name and quality, she felt, would be highly imprudent; but he implored so earnestly, yet with such diffidence; be had treated her with such respectful delicacy, while she was in his power unpro-tected; his manners were so noble; her obligations to him were so recent; and above all, her own inclination to see him again was so strong, that before she was herself aware of her intention, she hinted that she generally visited the Grotto of St. Hildegarde about two hours before sunset. The youth pressed her hand to his lips with respectful gratitude, breathed a fervent prayer for her welfare, and she then hastened into the castle, her cheeks glowing with blushes and her heart beating high with hope.

To one interview another still succeeded, and still did the unknown knight acquire a greater influence over the heart of the innocent Blanche. That influence he chiefly exerted in efforts to eradicate her antipathy to everything belonging to Frankheim; but he found it a less easy task to destroy her ill opinion of his relations than to inspire her with a favorable one of himself.

However, his own interest in her heart appeared to be so firmly established that he no longer dreaded lest the knowledge of his connections should make him the object of Blanche's aversion; and when the Palatine's summons compelled him to lead his retainers to Heidelberg, he gave his mistress at parting a solemn promise that when next they met, he would disclose to her his real name and situation; a secret which she was most anxious to know, and to arrive at which, she had exhausted all the little arts of which she was mistress, though all were exhausted in vain.

However, he had assured her of his rank being equal to her own; and the splendor of his dress, at once simple and magnificent, and (still more) the variety of his accomplishments and dignified frankness of his manners, convinced her that the sphere in which he moved must needs be elevated.

Such was the present situation of the lovers which Osbright now laid before the good Sir Lennard. His host heard him with evident satisfaction; and his excellent heart exulted in the prospect of a reconciliation between two families, the chiefs of which had both been his earliest friends, and with whom (in despite of their disunion) he was still upon the most amicable terms.

He therefore said everything in his power to confirm Osbright in his attachment. He exclaimed loudly against the injustice of supposing Gustavus to be concerned in the death of Joscelyn; he described him as the most humane of mortals, a man whose fault was rather to push compassion and benevolence beyond the limits of reason and prudence than to be seduced into the commission of a crime so atrocious as the murder of an unoffending child; and as to the tempta-tion which was supposed to have influenced Gustavus in this transaction, he quoted a thousand acts of disinterestedness and generosity, each strong enough to convince even the most prejudiced, that the man who performed them must possess a mind totally free from the pollution of avarice. In conclusion Sir Lennard promised the youth his best offices; and as he judged it most advisable to make the whole business known to Gustavus as soon as possible, he engaged to visit the castle of Orrenberg the next day, where he was certain that Osbright's proposals would be received with eagerness. The great point, however, was to remove from Rudiger's mind the persuasion that Gustavus had caused his younger son to be assassinated, and he advised Osbright to spare no pains to discover the real murderers; that mystery once cleared up, all other difficulties he looked upon as trifles. Osbright received Sir Lennard's advice with gratitude, promised to obey it implicitly, and having passed the night at his friend's castle, he returned with renovated hopes to the Chapel of St. John.

Father Peter gave him the most cordial welcome, though still ignorant that his humble cell was honored by affording a refuge to the heir of Frankheim. Osbright made him repeat the story of the murder circumstantially, and among other things the old man mentioned that the little finger of Joscelyn's left hand was missing when his corpse was found, and that it had been repeatedly sought on the fatal spot, but without success. This circumstance struck Osbright as very singular, and he thought it not impossible but that it might furnish a due to unravel the whole mystery. But with much more sanguine expectations did he learn from Father Peter that the assassin had left a wife, for whom (even while enduring the agony of the rack) he expressed the most ardent affec-tion.

Was it not probable then that this beloved wife was in her husband's confidence and could explain the motive which tempted him to commit the crime? Osbright resolved-to examine her himself; but he found that she had gone to visit a relation at some distance, where she was said to be inconsolable for the loss of her ill-fated husband. To depart without seeing Blanche was too much to be expected; he therefore determined to pass the day in Father Peter's cell, to visit St.

Hildegarde's Grotto in the evening, and after assuring himself that the heart of Blanche was still his own, to set forward on his expedition without suffering a moment's longer delay.

Evening approached; and Osbright was crossing the aisle which led toward the principal gate of the chapel when his attention was arrested by the murmuring of a voice, proceeding from a small oratory dedicated to the Virgin. The door was open, and he cast a passing glance within. A youth was kneeling at the shrine in fervent prayer, and a second glance assured Osbright that the youth was the page, Eugene.

Enthusiasm seemed to have marked Eugene for her own, even from his earliest infancy; and succeeding events had given to that enthusiasm a universal cast of tender melancholy. Rudiger esteemed and admired the Lady Magdalena; but a visit to the Convent of St. Hildegarde several years after his marriage convinced him that he had never loved till then. He there saw a sister of the order who made upon his heart the most forcible impression; and though Rudiger possessed many noble qualities, the mastery of his passions was not numbered among them. The personal attractions which had gained for him the heart of Magdalena were equally triumphant over the principles of the Sister Agatha; she eloped with him from the convent, and became the mother of Eugene.

But all the blandishments of her—seducer, whose love survived the gratification of his desires, could not stifle in her bosom the cries of remorse. She saw herself the disgrace of her noble family, and the violator of the sacred marriage-bed; the dread of discovery constantly tormented her; her perjury to Heaven made her look upon herself as a mark for divine vengeance; she trembled every moment with apprehension of punishment in this world, and she despaired of obtaining pardon in the next. At length her mental sufferings became too exquisite for endurance; she resolved to break the disgraceful chains which united her to Rudiger and endeavor to atone for her past errors by the penitence of her future life. She made by letter a full confession to the Lady Magdalena; entreated pardon for herself and protection for her helpless infant; and then hastened to conceal her ignominy in a retreat, to discover which baffled all the inquiries of her forsaken seducer.

Magdalena forgave her husband's faults, pitied his sufferings, and became the benevolent protectress of his child. It was thought highly advisable for the sake of his own respectability that Rudiger should be supposed to have no concern in this business, and that the disgraceful circumstances attending the child's birth should be suppressed as much as possible. Accordingly, Eugene was educated as a foundling, whose helpless situation had attracted Magdalena's notice and compassion; but this fortunate delusion was not suffered to last. The wretched mother felt that her end was approaching and could not resist her desire to see and bless her child, though she prudently resolved to keep her relation to him still unknown.

Remorse, and self-enforced penance the most cruel, had worn her to the very bone. Oppressed with long travel, her feet bleeding, fainting, dying, she arrived at the castle of Frankheim. She sought out her boy; she saw him; and in an agony of tenderness and grief the mother's heart betrayed her secret. The boy's character had ever appeared singular. He entered into no childish sports; he would listen for hours to stories of murders, or robbers, but above all he delighted in the narrative of religious miracles and the sufferings of martyrs. His favorite walk was in the churchyard, where he passed whole evenings, learning by heart the rhymes engraved upon the tombstones. He was seldom moved to laughter; even in his smile there was something melancholy; nor had he any way of expressing joy or gratitude, except by tears. Every word, look, and gesture already betrayed the enthusiast; and from his fondness for all church ceremonies and his continually chanting religious hymns, he had obtained among the domestics of Frankheim the name of the Little Abbot.

Such was the boy, who at ten years old saw himself unexpectedly clasped in the arms of an expiring mother, whom he had long numbered among the dead. The sudden recognition; her wild and emaciated appearance; her tattered garments, her bleeding feet; the passion of her kisses, the agony of her tears; the description of her faults, of her remorse, of her terrors of the future, of her dreadful and unexampled penance; all these united were too much for Eugene's sensibility to endure! When in spite of all Magdalena's efforts to prolong her existence, the wretched mother breathed her last, the son was forcibly torn from the corpse delirious.

No sooner had the report reached the Countess that a dying beggar had declared herself to be Eugene's mother than she hastened to assist the sufferer and rescue the feeling child from a scene so terrible. But she arrived too late; a few moments terminated the nun's existence, and Eugene had already received a shock, which during a twelvemonth set the physician's skill at defiance.

His senses at length returned; but his heart never seemed to recover from the wound, which had agonized it so exquisitely. Pale, drooping, absorbed in thought, nothing seemed capable of affording him pleasure. He declined all amusements; he neglected all attainments, both literary and warlike: and when chided by the chaplain for inattention to his lessons, and when mocked by the military vassals for effeminacy, he listened to their reproofs and taunts with indifference and answered both with silence. His time was passed in listless indolence; he would stand hour after hour dropping pebbles in the river and gazing upon the circles as they formed themselves and then vanished into nothing. Vain were the exertions of Magdalena and her husband to awaken him from this torpor of the mind; though compelled to endure their kindness, he evidently felt it a burden, and sedulously avoided it. Agatha's sad story occupied his whole soul; he could not but consider Magdalena as filling the place which his mother should have occupied; he could not but consider Rudiger as the author of his mother's sufferings; and though the Count almost doted upon the boy with a truly paternal tenderness, the most that he could obtain from him was implicit submission and cold respect.

Eugene only saw in himself a forlorn being, whose odious birth had branded his mother with infamy, and whose existence was given under circumstances too disgraceful to permit his being avowed by his surviving parent. Magdalena's kindness was the offspring of mere compassion; the memory of his mother's wrongs was inseparably connected with the sight of his father: he felt that he had no claim to the love of anyone, nor did he see anyone toward whom his heart felt love, till accident made him the preserver of the little Joscelyn. The child had strayed from its careless nurse, and fell into the river. No one but Eugene saw its danger, who having obstinately refused to practice all manly exercises was totally ignorant of the art of swimming. The river was deep, the stream was strong; to attempt to save Joscelyn was to expose himself to equal danger; yet without a moment's hesitation did the effeminate Eugene plunge into the river, grasp the child's garments with one hand and the bough of a neighbor. ing willow with the other; and thus did he sustain his already insensible burden, till his frantic cries attracted the notice of the domestics. They hastened to the place, and arriving at the very moment when the bough giving way menaced the child and his preserver with inevitable destruction.

From that moment Joscelyn became the object of Eugene's whole solicitude and affection. He was his brother, was a being who had no faults in his eyes, and was one who but for him would have been numbered with the dead. Attachment to Joscelyn now divided his heart with grief for the earthly sufferings of his mother and with religious terrors for her eternal salvation. However, as he increased in years, it was suspected in the castle, that other passions would ere long possess no inconsiderable influence over his bosom. Though he still shunned society, it was remarked that he only shunned that of men; in the company of women, his habitual gloom seemed to melt into a voluptuous languor. The Countess's damsels perceived that when they addressed him in the language of kindness, his large eyes swam in tears and sparkled with fire, and the rush of blood spread a hectic crimson over his pale fair cheeks. Moreover it was observed that, though his devotions were performed with unabated ardor, after he reached the age of fifteen Eugene prayed to no saints but female ones.

Even now it was to the Virgin that he was kneeling when Osbright discovered him in the oratory. During his short visits at Frankheim, the knight's attention had been engaged by the singularity of the page's demeanor; and though respect for his own character had induced Rudiger to conceal the relationship between himself and Eugene from his son's knowledge, still Osbright, prompted by his own feelings, had neglected no means of showing the boy that he bore him much good-will. But his advances were all rejected with the most obstinate coldness; Eugene only looked upon him as the possessor of that place which, if his own mother had filled Magdalena's, he should himself have occupied; he could not help envying Count Rudiger's fortunate heir and avowed offspring; and when he reflected that but for this odious elder brother his darling Joscelyn would one day be lord of the extensive domains of Frankheim, a sentiment mingled itself with his envy and repugnance, which nothing but his religious principles prevented from becoming hatred. As a Christian, he would not hate anyone; but as a human being, he felt that it was impossible for him to love Count Rudiger's eldest son and Joscelyn's elder brother.

Finding his attentions so ill repaid, Osbright bestowed no further thought on the wayward lad; and the interest with which he at this moment surveyed him arose from the recollection of Eugene's ardent attachment to the murdered child. He listened in mournful silence while the page poured forth his lamentations in a strain of devotion the most ardent; with a thousand touching expressions, with enthusiasm almost delirious, he described his favorite's perfections, and bewailed his own irreparable loss; but what was the knight's astonishment to hear the page conclude his orisons by imploring the blessed spirit of Joscelyn to protect from every danger and watch with celestial care the precious life of Blanche of Orrenberg!

An exclamation of surprise burst from Osbright's lips, and warned Eugene of his being overheard. The page started from the ground, and in his confusion a rosary formed of ebony and coral escaped from his hands. Osbright sprang forward, and seized it, for he knew that rosary well; and had he doubted its identity, the name of Blanche engraved upon the golden crucifix would have removed all hesitation on the subject; in an instant a thousand jealous fears rushed before his fancy. The lad was singularly beautiful; his figure, light and exquisitely formed, might have served the statuary as a model for a zephyr;7 confusion had spread over his cheeks an unusual glow, and his bright and flowing hair glittered in the sunbeams like dark, gold. Osbright eyed him with displeasure and asked him haughtily how that rosary came into his hands.

"Noble sir," replied Eugene, trembling and embarrassed; "I... I found it.—I found it near the caves of St. Hildegarde."

"And of course you know not its owner, or I should not find it still in your possession?"—-(Eugene was silent.)

7 In classical mythology, the west wind, son of Aeolus and Aurora.."Well! the workmanship pleases me; there is a diamond of price; take it, Eugene, and let the rosary be mine."

He drew a ring from his finger, and presented it to the page; but it was not accepted.

"Oh! Sir Osbright," exclaimed Eugene, and sank upon his knee; "take my life from me; it is at your disposal; but while I live, do not deprive me of that rosary. It is my only remembrance of an event so dear to me... Of the day in which I first found existence valuable!—Three months are passed, since while following my lord, your father, to the chase, my horse became ungovernable and bore me to the brink of a precipice. My efforts to restrain him were in vain. I at length sprang from his back, but too late to save myself. I rolled down the declivity and was dashed to the bottom of the precipice. I lost my senses, but projecting shrubs doubtless broke my descent and preserved me from destruction. On opening my eyes, I believed that my fall had killed me and that I was in Heaven already; for near me knelt a form so angelic, with looks so benevolent, with eyes so expressive of compassion! And she questioned me about my safety in so sweet a voice!"

"And she related with an air of such interest, how in returning from St. Hildegarde's Grotto she had observed my fall; how she had trembled for my life, and had brought water from the cave to wash off the blood, and had torn her veil to bind up my wounded head! And then, she bade me so tenderly be of good cheer, for that the danger was passed, and that she hoped I should soon be quite well! Oh! How valuable did my life then become in my own eyes when I found that it had some worth in hers!"

"And you knew not her name?"

"Oh! no, my lord, not then; but alas! her terror too soon made me guess it; for no sooner did I mention the castle of Frankheim as my abode, then she uttered a loud shriek, started from the ground with every mark of horror and alarm, and fled from me with the rapidity of an arrow."

"Then did my foreboding heart tell me too truly that she, in whom the bare mention of Frankheim could excite such aversion, must needs belong to the hostile family of Orrenberg. That suspicion was confirmed when I observed lying near me this rosary, which she had forgotten in her haste, and whose crucifix bears the dear, dear name of Blanche!—a name, which from that moment I blessed in every prayer! A name, which has ever since been held in my fancy sacred as that of my patron saint!"

"And you saw her no more? And you spoke to her no more? Nay, answer me with frankness, boy, or I swear..."

"Oh! be patient, good my lord; I mean not to deceive you. Yes; once more, only once I addressed her; I would have restored her rosary; I wished to thank her for her timely succor; but the moment that she beheld me, her former terrors returned. She shrieked out 'a Frankheimer!' and hastened away, as if flying from an assassin. Thenceforward I accosted her no more. I found that the sight of me alarmed her, and I forbode to intrude upon her, whom my whole soul adores, a presence so hateful! You now know all; noble knight, restore my rosary."

The frankness of this narration dissipated entirely Osbright's jealous terrors. The impassioned yet respectful manner, in which Blanche was mentioned, and the height of admiration which the sight of her had inspired, both pleased and softened him; and he could not help feeling himself strongly influenced in favor of the young enthusiast, whose heart beat so perfectly in unison with his own. Yet he judged it prudent to conceal that favorable impression and accompany the surrender of the rosary with a lecture on the folly of his nourishing so hopeless a passion.

"There is your rosary," said he, assuming a severity of tone and manner very foreign to his feelings; "though I know not, whether in restoring it I do you any kindness. Imprudent youth, for whom do you feel this excess of adoration? For the daughter of your patron's most inveterate enemy; of a man accused of the murder of your dearest friend; of one against whom scarce forty hours ago you vowed in this very chapel..."

"Oh! No, no, no!" exclaimed the page with a look of horror. "I vowed nothing; I took no oath; I heard, but joined not in the blasphemy; and when all around me cursed the devoted family of Orrenberg, I prayed, for the angel Blanche!"

"For the daughter of Joscelyn's supposed assassin? Joscelyn, whom you professed to love so truly, that your life..."

"Oh! and I did love Joscelyn, truly, dearly! But I feel that I love Blanche even better than Joscelyn, a thousand, oh! and a thousand times!"

"Love her indeed? Alas, poor youth! Love whom? The only child of the rich and noble Count of Orrenberg; after me, the heiress of all those domains, on which you have been educated through my father's charity. Blanche, Countess of Orrenberg, and the orphan page, Eugene, a foundling, without family, without friend; how ill do these names sound together! My good lad, I mean not to wound your feelings, but observe, how hopeless is your present pursuit; rouse yourself from your romantic dream, and erase from your heart this frantic passion!"

During this speech, the glow faded from the cheeks of Eugene; the fire of enthusiasm no longer blazed in his eyes; the deepest gloom of melancholy overspread his countenance. His head sank upon his bosom, and his eyes were filled with tears.

"True! true! sir knight," said he after a short pause. "I know it well! I am an orphan boy, without family, without friends! God help me!"

He pressed the crucifix to his trembling lips, bowed his head to Osbright with humility, and turned to leave the chapel.

Osbright was deeply affected, and he suffered him to pass him in silence; but soon recollecting himself. "Stay, Eugene," said he, calling after him, and the page stopped. "I would not have my parents know that I am in their neighborhood; should you reveal that I am here, my displeasure..."

"I reveal?" interrupted Eugene proudly. "I am no tale-bearer, sir knight!"—and he quitted the chapel, his passion for Blanche inflamed by the opposition made to it, and his antipathy to Osbright strengthened by resentment at his being the person who opposed it.

CHAPTER VI

—"My life! my soul! my all that Heaven can give!
Death's life with thee, without thee death to live!"
Dryden.

While Osbright was employed in smoothing the real obstacles to their union, his mistress was the victim of imaginary terror. She had discovered in her unknown lover the son of her father's most inveterate enemy; a man too, whom from her cradle she had been taught to consider with horror, and who (according to Sir Ottokar's account) had taken a most solemn and irrevocable oath to exterminate herself and her whole family. She now believed that Osbright's protestations were all false and only calculated to beguile her to destruction; or else that he was ignorant of her origin, when he pretended affection; or that, even if in spite of her bearing the detested name of Orrenberg, he had still formerly felt a real love for her, she doubted not that grief for his brother's murder and thirst of vengeance had converted that love into hatred, and that he would seize the first opportunity of fulfilling his horrible vow by plunging his dagger in her bosom..But she prudently resolved to afford him no such opportunity. The image of her loved preserver no longer beckoned her to the grotto; she only saw there him whom her prejudiced fancy had delighted to load with every vice, and who thirsted to sign in her blood his claim to the rich inheritance of her parents. No! To St. Hildegarde's Grotto she would venture no more; that was a point determined! And it remained determined for a whole long day and night; but when the second morning arrived, her resolution faltered; and when the evening was at hand, her prudence totally failed. Yet another hour, and the knight would be waiting for her in the cave; and for what purpose he waited now appeared to her but of little consequence. He might murder her, it's true; but to see him no more, she felt, was but to perish by a more painful though more lingering death, and she determined to ascertain the worst immediately. Her mother was occupied by household arrangements. Gustavus was in close conference with Sir Lennard of Kleeborn, who was just arrived; no one observed her movements, and she employed her liberty in hastening to the Grotto of St. Hildegarde.

No one was there; and now a new terror seized her, lest Osbright should not mean to come. She seated herself on a broken stone which had rolled from the rock above, and was lost in melancholy reflections when someone took her hand gently. She looked up; Osbright stood before her; but in the moment of surprise she only saw in him the dreaded assassin, and uttering a cry of terror, her first movement was to fly from the place. The knight started back in astonishment. But she soon recollected herself, and returned.

"Is it you then?" she said, endeavoring to assume a tranquil look, and extending her hand with a smile, equally expressive of tenderness and melancholy; "I feared... I thought..."

"What did you think? What could your innocence have to fear?" And he gently drew her back to the seat which she had quitted and took his place by her side.

"I feared... that some enemy... that some assassin... that some emissary of the Count of Frankheim..."

"Ah! Blanche! Still this aversion? To belong to Frankheim is sufficient to become the object of your hate."

"All who belong to Frankheim hate me."

"Not all, Blanche, certainly."

"The Count at least."

"Dearest Blanche! did you but know the pain which I feel when you calumniate the Count...! He is stern and passionate I confess, but he has ever been an honorable man. Shall I own to you the truth, my Blanche? The Count is my friend, is my best friend! His affection is my proudest boast; his commands I have never disobeyed..."

"Indeed?—and never will?"

"Never; at least, I hope not! His commands from my earliest infancy have ever been to me as a law, and... my love! why thus pale? What alarms you? What distresses you?"

"'Tis nothing! It will soon be past! I am not quite well, and..."

"You speak still more faintly! Stay one moment! I will bring water for you from the grotto."

"Oh! no, no, no!" she exclaimed, and detained him by his arm. He stopped, surprised at the eagerness with which she spoke. "Yet 'tis no matter!" she continued; "bring it, if you will; I will drink it."

"I will return instantly!" said he, and hastened to the waterfall. Blanche started wildly from her seat; she sank upon her knees, covered her face with her hands, and prayed for a few moments fervently and silently.."Now then," she said in a firm voice, while she rose from the ground; "now then I am prepared for everything. Let him bring me what he will, be it water or be it poison, from his hands will I receive it without hesitation, and die, if he will have it so, without a murmur."

A consecrated goblet ever stood upon the rustic altar of St. Hildegarde; it was supposed to be that, which had once pressed the blessed lips of the saint, and even the starving robber respected its sanctity. Osbright hastily filled it, and returning to his mistress, urged her to taste the water which it contained.

Blanche received the cup with a trembling hand, and fixing her eyes upon his countenance.

"Will it not chill me too suddenly?" she asked.

"You need not drink much of it; a few drops will be sufficient to produce the effect desired."

"Indeed? Is it so powerful then? Nay, it is all the better. See, sir knight, you are obeyed; from your hands even this is welcome!" And she placed the goblet to her lips, nor doubted that she drank a farewell to the world. "Look!" she resumed restoring the cup; "have I swallowed enough? Are you satisfied?"

"Blanche!" exclaimed the youth, his surprise at her demeanor increasing with every moment; "what is the matter? What means this mysterious conduct? You seem to me so much altered..."

"Already? Does it then work so speedily? Nay, then I must be sudden, and here all disguise shall end. You promised, when I saw you last, that at our next meeting you would disclose your name. I know it already, Osbright of Frankheim; know the hatred which you bear to me and mine; know the dreadful oath which was taken last night in the chapel of St. John, and know also that you have now made one step toward fulfilling it. Osbright, when I raised yonder goblet to my lips, I was not ignorant that it contained poison ..."

"Poison?" interrupted Osbright. "What! you believe then... you suspect... yet believe it still! Yes, Blanche, yes! Let this convince you that the cup which you have tasted, Osbright will raise to his lips with joy, even though that cup be poisoned!"—and he seized the goblet, and drank its contents with eagerness.

"Osbright! My own Osbright!" exclaimed Blanche, and sank upon her lover's bosom. "Oh! that it were indeed poison, and that I might die with you in this moment, for to live with you I feel myself unworthy! Shame upon me! How could I for one instant belie your generous nature so grossly! Never, no, never more will I suspect..."

"Nor me, nor any one, my Blanche, I hope, without some better reason. Oh! banish from your bosom the gloomy fiend, Mistrust; so pure a shrine should never be polluted by an inmate so odious! Away with the prejudices, which have been so carefully instilled into your youthful mind; see no more with the eyes of parents; see with your own, my Blanche, and judge by your own good heart of the feelings of others. Then will the world again become lovely in your

54

sight, for you will see it the abode of truth, of virtue, of affection; then will this host of imagined enemies be converted into a band of real friends; then will your mind be freed from these visionary terrors, so injurious to others, so painful to yourself, which now fill your waking thoughts with anxiety and your nightly dreams with gloomy recollections. You have told me yourself, that you have frequently started from sleep exclaiming that Count Rudiger of Frankheim was at hand; and yet this Count Rudiger is Osbright's father! You have mistaken me; you are mistaken in him, and...?"

"In the Count? Oh! no, no, no, Osbright! Impossible! Indeed, indeed the Count is a very fierce, a very cruel man! ah! your partiality blinds you; but if you knew as well as I do... but I was forbidden to mention it...?"

"And have you still secrets from me, Blanche? From this moment I have none to you."

"Nay, look not so sad; you shall know all; and you should have known it before, but that you ever spoke so warmly in favor of the Count that I was unwilling to grieve you. Well then, Osbright; it is certain (quite certain!) that the Count of Frankheim caused my poor brother Philip to be poisoned."

"Indeed? Quite certain? And do you know, Blanche, that it is equally certain, nay, much more certain, that the Count of Orrenberg caused my brother to be assassinated in Burnholm wood?"

"Oh! most atrocious calumny! Oh! Falsehood most incredible! What! My father, whose actions..."

"My father never did an unworthy action, either, Blanche."

"Nay, but I saw with my own eyes the livid spots with which Philip's neck—I too saw with mine the deep wound which gaped on poor Joscelyn's bosom."

"The attendants, the physician, all have told me themselves..."

"Every inmate of Frankheim Castle heard the confession..."

"That your father had bribed Philip's nurse, who left us about a week before his illness..."

"That assassins were bribed by your father to murder Joscelyn while hunting."

"Nay, what is more strong, my mother herself assured me..."

"But what is still stronger than that is that your father's crime was actually confessed by the very assassins themselves."

"Well, Osbright, your surely cannot expect me to see everything with your eyes..."

"Should I see everything with yours, Blanche?"

"Nor to believe my dear good father, whose heart I know so well, guilty of a crime so base and so atrocious!"

"Does not the argument hold equally good for me, Blanche? Your father may be innocent of Joscelyn's death, but so is mine of Philip's; you love your father well, but not better than I love mine. Each thinks the other's father to be guilty; why may not each be wrong? Both believe their own father to be innocent, and why should not both be right?"

"Oh! that it were so! How gladly should I banish from my bosom these gloomy terrors which now torture it so cruelly. No, Osbright; the heart may feel, but the tongue can never utter, how painful it is for me to hate one who is so much beloved by you!"

Osbright thanked her by a kiss, the purest and the warmest that ever was sealed upon the lip of woman; and he now proceeded to unfold to her his intentions of seeking the widow of the assassin, and endeavoring to learn from her the real motives of her husband for murdering the innocent Joscelyn. She approved of his design, and then urged his immediate departure, as the evening was already closing round them and Osbright's road lay through a forest rendered dangerous in several parts by pit-falls and not entirely free from wild beasts. Osbright obeyed; but he first advised her to visit St. Hildegarde's Grotto no more till his return, of which he could easily apprise her by means of Sir Lennard of Kleeborn.

"For I must confess," he added, "though I am certain, that nothing could induce my father to act ill deliberately, yet his passions are so violent, and so frequently overcome his better judgment, that I know not what extremes he might be hurried in a momentary ebullition of fury. My brother's death (I understand) has almost driven him frantic; he breathes vengeance against the whole family of Orrenberg; it is rumored also that the herald whom he dispatched to signify to your father..."

"Alas! It is but too true! The wild cruel people murdered the poor man; but my father did his utmost to prevent the crime; indeed, indeed, Osbright, my father was not in fault!"

"Heaven grant that it may be found so; but at present appearances are greatly against Count Gustavus, and this unlucky event will make my father's resentment burn with ten-fold fury. He is noble, generous, benevolent, friendly... But in his rage he is terrible, and he cherishes in his heart with unjustifiable fondness the thirst for vengeance. Some officious vassal may observe your visits hither, and unprotected as you are, may easily purchase his lord's favor by delivering you into his power. Dearest Blanche, enraged as he is at this moment, I would not even answer that your life..."

"Mine? One, who never offended him by word or deed? One, who for your sake would so willingly love him? And you really think... Ah! Osbright, say what you will, I fear that your father is a very wicked man!"

"He has his faults, but they are greatly overbalanced by his virtues. Yet I confess... there have been moments when... But let us drop this unpleasant subject. Time presses; I must be gone. Give me your promise not to visit this spot during my absence, one sweet kiss to confirm that promise, and then farewell, my Blanche."

The promise was given; the kiss was taken; the farewell was said; and then Osbright, having conducted his mistress in safety to the spot which concealed the private entrance to Orrenberg Castle (and which was within a very short distance of the cave) returned to the place, where he had fastened his courser, and giving him the spur, was soon concealed within the shades of the neighboring forest.

But scarcely had he quitted her, when Blanche recollected that the consecrated goblet was left on the outside of the cave. To replace this, her reverence for the saint made her think absolutely necessary; yet the close of her conversation with Osbright made her feel no small degree of repugnance to revisiting the grotto by herself. However, it was so near that she could not suppose it possible for her to meet with any danger during the few minutes which it would take her to perform this duty, and therefore after some little hesitation she retraced her steps.

Trembling as she ran, she traversed the space which divided her from the cave, threaded the rocky passages, and soon reached the mouth of the cave. The goblet was replaced; an Ave was murmured before the altar in all haste, and she now hurried back again; when as she rushed out of the grotto—"Stay!"—exclaimed a voice, and springing from the rock above, a man stood before her. She shrieked and started back; the moon, which was now risen, showed her what seemed rather to be a specter than any mortal being. His tall thin form (viewed through the medium of her fears and seen but indistinctly among the shadows of the surrounding rocks) dilated to a height which appeared gigantic, his tresses fluttering wildly in the evening blast, his limbs trembling with agitation, his face colorless as the face of a corpse, his large eyes almost starting from their sockets and glaring with all the fires of delirium, his hands filled with locks of bright hair torn from his own head, and stained with blood which had flowed from his own self-mangled bosom, such was the stranger; such was the wretched Eugene.

The terror which the sight of him evidently caused in Blanche had prevented the page from obtruding his presence upon her any more; but he could not prevail upon himself to abstain from the delight of gazing upon that beauty which had made so forcible an impression upon his youthful heart. He watched her and observed that regularly every evening she visited the cave of St. Hildegarde; and regularly every evening did Eugene climb the rocks among which it was situated, and feed his hopeless passion by gazing for whole hours upon the lovely form of Blanche. He admired the celestial expression of her countenance, as she knelt in prayer before the shrine; he listened in silent ecstasy, when, seated before the grotto's mouth and weaving into garlands the wildflowers which sprouted among the rocks, she chanted some sweet though simple ballad; he smiled, when he saw her smile at the dexterity with which her flowery work had been completed; and when some melancholy thought glanced across her mind, he echoed back the sigh which escaped from her bosom. He knew not that the wreaths were woven to deck the seat which had been hallowed by sustaining a rival; he knew not that the sigh proceeded from grief for that rival's absence.

And thus had whole months rolled away; and with every day did the charms of Blanche inflame his heart with more glowing passion and exalt his imagination to a higher pitch of enthusiasm. At length came the fatal blow which at once destroyed this solitary source of ideal happiness; he found not only that he had a beloved rival, but that this rival was the man who possessed that place in his father's affections which he would so gladly have possessed in them himself; was Count Rudiger's avowed offspring, while he was rejected and pointed out to the world as nothing better than an orphan and an outcast; was the heir of the rich domains of Frankheim, while he was condemned to a life of servitude and obscurity; in short, was the very man toward whom of all existing beings he cherished, and had cherished from his childhood, the most inveterate and uncontrollable antipathy.

Breathless with agitation, and fixing his nails in his bosom in order to distract the sense of mental agony by the infliction of bodily pain, he had witnessed from the rock above them the interview between the lovers. He heard not their words; but he saw, as they sat, the arm of Osbright tenderly encircling the waist of Blanche, and witnessed the kiss which he pressed upon her lips at parting. They were gone; yet the boy still lay extended upon the rock, stupefied by a blow so unexpected. A few minutes restored him to sensation, but not to himself. Horror at Josedyn's death had shaken his nerves most cruelly; since that event grief had scarcely permitted his tasting food; that constitutional infirmity which the knowledge of his mother's sad story had inflamed into delirium now exerted itself with dreadful violence upon his enfeebled frame and exalted imagination; his brain was unable to support the shock, and he now stood a maniac before the affrighted Blanche.

"It is she indeed!" he exclaimed. "She here again? Here, and alone! Oh! Then it was no illusion! The night-wind murmured in my ear— 'death!'—And the screech-owl shrieked in my ear—'death!'—And the wind and the screech-owl told me true, for you are returned on purpose! Yes, yes; I feel it well, angel; you are here, and the hour is come!"

"What hour? I know you not. You terrify me."

She attempted to pass him, but he grasped her by the wrist. "Terrified? Are you not a blessed spirit, and what can you fear? I must away to the skies, and there will I kneel and implore for you and pray that you may speedily follow me thither! You will soon be made a saint in Heaven, but I must prepare the way for you; take this sword, and plunge it... Nay, nay! Why should you dread to use it? Have you not plunged a dagger in my heart already? You have, you have! And oh! That wound was a wound so painful... Take it, I say; take it; here is my naked bosom!"

And as he said this, he tore open his doublet with one hand, while with frantic eagerness he endeavored to force her to take the sword with the other; when summoning up all her strength Blanche rushed swiftly past him, and with loud shrieks fled through the rocky passage. The frantic youth pursued her, in vain imploring her to stay; with fruitless efforts did Blanche exert her speed; the maniac gained upon her; and overcome by terror she fell breathless at his feet, at the moment when guided by her shrieks Baron Ottokar arrived to her assistance. He heard her scream for help; he saw her pursued by one who held an unsheathed sword; he beheld her sink upon the earth and doubted not that she had perished by the blow of an assassin.."Inhuman ruffian!" exclaimed the knight, and instantly his sword struck the supposed murderer to the earth. Then raising the trembling Blanche in his arms, he hastened toward the castle to procure surgical assistance for his lovely burden.

During Blanche's absence, Sir Lennard of Kleeborn was employed in the performance of his promise to Osbright. He requested an audience of the Count of Orrenberg, which was readily granted; but Gustavus added that as what Sir Lennard had to state was announced to be of importance, he begged that Baron Ottokar might share the communication; the nature of his engagements to that young nobleman being such that they possessed a common interest in everything. Sir Lennard foreboded from this declaration an obstacle to his negotiation; however, he immediately commenced it, disclosed to the astonished Count the mutual attachment between Osbright and his daughter, and concluded by advising him most strenuously to seize so favorable an opportunity of putting a final close to the disputes which had so long separated the kindred houses of Orrenberg and Frankheim.

While Gustavus listened to this narrative, a variety of emotions expressed themselves by turns on his countenance. Sir Lennard had finished. The Count passed a few minutes in silence; but at length taking his resolution decisively, he assured Sir Lennard, that most earnestly did he desire to see amity established between the two families; that there was no personal sacrifice which he would not joyfully make to accomplish an event so desirable; but that unfortunately, he had already contracted such engagements as formed an insuperable obstacle to the union of Blanche and Osbright.

"No, my lord," hastily interrupted Ottokar; "you have contracted none, at least if you allude to those which you have contracted with me. It is true, last night I received your knightly word that the hand of Blanche should be mine; and had you promised me the Imperial crown, I should have thought the boon less valuable. But when the object is, to prevent the effusion of kindred blood, to establish peace between the two noblest families in the whole Palatinate, nay more, to procure the happiness of Blanche herself, shall I suffer my own selfish wishes to interfere? Shall I hesitate for one moment to sacrifice them to the general welfare? No, my lord, read the heart of Ottokar more justly. Were the affections of your daughter the prize, I would dispute it against Osbright, against the world, and would never resign my claim but with the last sigh of my bosom; but the possession of her hand alone could only make me wretched. The heart of Blanche is Osbright's; Blanche can only be happy in being his, and unless she is happy, I must be miserable myself. Count of Orrenberg, I restore your promise; I resume my own; let this wished-for union take place. Heaven itself surely lighted up this flame in the bosoms of the lovers; and the hour which gives Blanche to the envied Osbright will doubtless bury in eternal oblivion all past offenses, all existing prejudices, all future mistrust. It is true, my heart will bleed; but the applause of my conscience will repay me for every selfish pang most amply. Still consider me as your warmest friend, Gustavus; but for the sake of Blanche, I must now refuse to be your son."

In vain did Gustavus combat this generous resignation. Ottokar was firm, and at length the Count honestly confessed to Sir Lennard the joy which he should feel at the accomplishment of the union in question. The difficulty now was how to convince Rudiger of the injustice of his suspicions respecting Joscelyn's murder, and to bring him to view Osbright's attachment in the same favorable light. In this also Ottokar proffered his assistance. As nephew to the Lady Magdalena, though he was no favorite with her lord, he had ready access to the castle of Frankheim; that lady was well aware of the strength of his attachment to Blanche, and the generosity of her own nature rendered her fully capable of appreciating the sacrifice which he made in surrendering his claims in favor of Osbright's. He knew also that the feuds between the families had long been to her a source of mental uneasiness the most acute; that she had ever vindicated the conduct of Gustavus, as far as Rudiger's violence would permit her prudence to give such an opinion; and he was certain, that she would seize with joy an opportunity of terminating disputes so odious. He therefore proposed his immediate departure for the castle of Frankheim, where he would make a confidential communication of the whole business to the Countess, and discuss with her the most likely means of gaining over to their side the inclinations of her stormy husband. This plan was universally approved of; and without an hour's delay Ottokar set out for Frankheim Castle, accompanied by the warmest gratitude of Gustavus, and the highest admiration of Sir Lennard.

It was on his progress to Frankheim that the shrieks of the alarmed Blanche had summoned him to her assistance. On his arrival with her at the castle, immediately all was anxiety and confusion; but it was soon ascertained that she had received no wound, though some time elapsed before she could recollect herself sufficiently to give an account of what had happened.

Even then, her narrative was greatly confused; alarm and anxiety to escape had prevented her from hearing much of what the maniac addressed to her. She could only relate, that a youth (whom she remembered to have seen twice before, and who had confessed himself to be a Frankheimer) had surprised her among the rocks; had accosted her with much violence and passion, frequently mentioning the word—"death"—and (as she believed) had told her that her hour was come. She was however quite certain that he accused her of having attempted "to plunge a dagger in his heart," had threatened "to make her a saint in Heaven," and had drawn his sword to put his threats in execution; at which she had fled, still pursued by him, till her strength failed her, and she sank on the earth before him. Having given this imperfect account, Blanche was committed to the care of her female attendants and advised by the physician to retire to rest, and endeavor to compose her ruffled spirits; advice, which she readily adopted, and immediately withdrew to her own apartment.

Gustavus had listened to her narrative with surprise, Ulrica with horror; and when Ottokar confirmed the assertion of Blanche that the supposed assassin was in the service of the Count of Frankheim (adding, that he had seen him occasionally in attendance upon Magdalena, and that he rather believed his name to be Eugene), the Countess darted a triumphant glance upon her husband. The latter ordered some domestics to go in quest of the assassin and convey him to the castle.

"Perhaps," said he, "his wound may not be mortal, and we may induce him to explain this mysterious business. I confess, that at present it wears a most hideous aspect; yet I cannot believe that the noble and brave Count Rudiger would descend to so base an action as to instigate a menial to take away the life of an innocent girl by assassination. If indeed, he should really be guilty of an action so atrocious..."

"If?" interrupted his wife impatiently. "And is it possible any longer to doubt his guilt? Is not everything confirmed? Does not this agree with my suspicions respecting Philip? Suspicions, did I say? 'Twas certainty! 'Twas fact, supported by proofs too clear to be mistaken by any eyes, but by those of wilful blindness! Nay, I could tell you more..."

"Indeed?" said Gustavus with a look of incredulity.

"Yes, Gustavus, yes! You remember well the fever which about two years ago brought you to the very gates of the sepulcher? You were recovering; you were pronounced out of danger; when a present of sweetmeats arrived for you from the Lady Magdalena."

"And what inference..."

"Be patient; I come to the point. I warned you not to taste them, and presented you with some conserves prepared by my own hand. You were obstinate; you first ridiculed my fears, then chided me for entertaining such unjust suspicions. What was the result? You ate freely of Magdalena's present, and the very next day your fever returned with such violence as made the physician for several days despair of your recovery."

"It was very singular! You are perfectly correct, Ulrica; and certainly... But stay! I think I recollect one little circumstance, which... Exactly so! Our dispute took place in the honeysuckle bower on the south-side of the garden, and out of patience at (what you termed) my obstinacy, you left me in displeasure. Scarcely were you gone, when old Grim the wolf-dog came bounding to caress me, and springing upon me unexpectedly, Magdalena's present fell from my hands, and the vessel broke into a thousand pieces. This accident made me have recourse to your conserves, which were still standing on the table; and what is something singular, old Grim (who had appropriated the fallen sweetmeats to himself without hesitation) suffered not the least inconvenience; while I had scarcely tasted those prepared by your own hand, before my fever returned with violence, and I was declared to be in danger of my life."

"Why, certainly," said Ulrica, hesitating and embarrassed, "there are two ways of telling everything. Appearances seemed strong... I argued to the best of my knowledge...Everybody is liable to be mistaken..."

"Are they so? Then, good Ulrica, since you find yourself mistaken in one instance, allow the possibility of your having been mistaken in another. In short, I insist upon it, and will not be disobeyed, that you are henceforth silent on the subject of Philip's malady. Were he poisoned or were he not, it is my pleasure that he should be mentioned only as dead, and nothing further."

"Nay, Ulrica! Not a syllable more, I entreat you!—My friends," he continued, turning to Ottokar and Sir Lennard, "advise me what to do. This new adventure, I own, wears a very embarrassing appearance; and yet appearances are no less strong against myself respecting the herald's death, and still more respecting the murder of young Joscelyn. One of my own people was found near the corpse; he declared upon the rack with his last breath that I had instigated him to commit the crime; and yet God sees the heart and knows that I am innocent. Rudiger may be equally guiltless of this attack upon my child; if fortunately, there should still be life in the assassin, and he could be brought to confess..."

"Nay," exclaimed Ottokar, "he must confess; he shall confess! If he refuses, the rack shall force from him..."

"And if he then declares that Rudiger set him on..."

"Then the business is ended! Then Rudiger's guilt is clear, and..."

"Indeed? Then it is also clear that I am Joscelyn's murderer. Is not that equally well proved, Sir Ottokar, and by means exactly the same?"

The youth colored, and hung his head in confusion; nor did any one break the silence, till a domestic entering informed the Count, that the assassin had been removed from the place where Sir Ottokar left him. On inquiry he had learned from some peasants that they had found the youth bleeding profusely, but that his wound appeared not to be dangerous; that they were preparing to convey him to the castle, when a party of Frankheimers accidently passed that way, and, recognizing a favorite domestic of their liege-lord, had forced him from them and hastened to convey him out of the domains of Orrenberg.

All hopes of Eugene's clearing up this mystery being thus removed, it was thought best that Ottokar should resume his intended visit to the Lady Magdalena, should inform her of all that had happened, should entreat her to account for the highly culpable conduct of the page, and ascertain whether Rudiger was disposed to bury all mutual injuries in oblivion; a measure which for his own part Gustavus professed himself still perfectly ready to adopt in spite of the suspicious transactions of that eventful evening. Ottokar immediately set forth; but Sir Lennard remained at the castle of Orrenberg to wait the issue of the young warrior's negotiation.

CHAPTER VII

—"The image of a wicked heinous fault lives in his eye;
that close aspect of his doth show the mood of a much troubled
bosom."—
King John.

The arrival of Ottokar at Frankheim Castle appeared to create no
trifling astonishment and embarrassment in the domestics. Suspicion
and ill-humor were expressed on every countenance; and Wilfred,
the seneschal,8 only answered the youth's inquiries for the Lady
Magdalena by a dry and sullen—"this way, sir knight!" The
Countess was alone; his appearance seemed to excite in her almost as
much surprise as it had produced on her attendants, and her
reception of him was studiously cold. But the frankness and
impetuosity of Ottokar's nature soon banished this constraint; he
opened his embassy without loss of time; and as she listened, the
countenance of his auditress gradually brightened.

The mutual attachment of Osbright and Blanche equally surprised
and pleased her; she bestowed the highest encomia on that
generosity of sentiment which had prompted Ottokar to sacrifice his
own passion to the general welfare; she declared her thorough
persuasion of the merits of the fair Blanche, and her anxiety to see
these odious feuds terminated in an amicable manner. She was also
willing to give credit to Ottokar's solemn protestations, that
Gustavus was innocent of Joscelyn's death; but she greatly feared
that it would be difficult to inspire her husband with the same
confidence; especially at the present moment when his persuasion of
Gustavus's animosity had gained additional strength from several
late occurrences. The account of the herald's murder, she said, had
inspired Rudiger with a degree of indignation, which (often as she
had witnessed the strength of his emotions) had far surpassed
anything, of which she had before believed him capable.

Ottokar hastened to clear up this transaction, at which he was
present; and his account perfectly exculpated Gustavus in

Magdalena's eyes, though (conscious of Rudiger's innate obstinacy) she was doubtful of its being equally successful with her husband. Ottokar, whose chief virtue was by no means that of patience, took fire at this; and it escaped him to say that it ill became a person to be so difficult in believing the innocence of another, who lay himself under such strong suspicions of having instigated an assassin to commit the very same crime. The Countess eagerly demanded an explanation and heard with surprise and resentment which increased with every word that in the course of that very evening a domestic of Count Rudiger had attempted to stab the Lady Blanche and would have succeeded in his diabolical attempt had not Ottokar arrived in time to fell the assassin to the ground.

Ottokar was still expatiating with all the warmth of a lover on the atrocity of the attempt; the Countess was still listening to this dreadful charge in such horror as deprived her of all power to interrupt her nephew; when the door was thrown open with violence, and Count Rudiger rushed into the room.

8 A major-domo for a medieval lord, generally his steward..

"Have you heard it, Magdalena?" he exclaimed in a thundering voice, while he stamped upon the floor with passion; "have you heard—at that moment his eyes rested upon Ottokar, and instantly they appeared to flash out fire. He started back; all the blood in his body seemed at once to rush into his face; for some moments he gazed upon the youth in terrific silence, as if he would have devoured him with his eyes. At length—So!" he exclaimed in a satisfied tone; "here! He is here!—What hoa! Wilfred!"—And he rushed again from the apartment, as abruptly as he had entered.

"What can this mean?" said the amazed and trembling Magdalena; "those looks... that well-known terrible expression... Oh! This very moment I must be satisfied."—She hastened to a window which overlooked the principal court, and summoned the old porter, who was then crossing it. He soon entered the apartment, and the Countess hastily inquired whether within the last hour any strangers had arrived at the castle and whether her lord had seen them.

"No, lady, no strangers!" replied the old man, "but truly Martin and his son Hans, the farmers of Helmstadt, are arrived, and sad news they bring to be sure. By your inquiry, lady, I suppose, that you have not yet heard what has happened at Orrenberg? Ah! the hard hearts! Ah! the barbarians! How could they be so cruel as to hurt the poor harmless innocent lad! One so gentle, that... the Lord have mercy! It is you, Sir Ottokar? Why, surely you must be distracted to show your face within these walls, after committing an act so barbarous!"

Ottokar declared his ignorance of the old man's meaning.

"Indeed? Nay, then perhaps the story is not true; Martin and Hans may have mistaken the name, and Heaven grant it may prove so! But to be plain, sir knight, Martin told me himself that on his road hither he found the young page Eugene bleeding and fainting; that the peasants who stood near him had assured him that the lad was stabbed by no hand but yours, and that you had perpetrated this barbarous action by the command of the Lady Blanche, under whose very eyes it was committed. Finding that Eugene still lived, and knowing how much my lord and yourself, noble lady, value him, Martin and his companions rescued him from the hands of the Orrenbergers, and endeavored to bring him home to the castle. But his wound being dangerous, they thought it safest to stop with him at the Convent of St. John, where they left him under the care of the good fathers, and then hastened hither to inform my lord of what had happened. But, bless my heart! I quite forget, lady; the Count ordered me to summon Wilfred immediately to his chamber, and I doubt, even this little delay will bring me into anger. Your pardon, lady; I must away this instant!"—And he hurried out of the apartment.

"Eugene?" repeated Magdalena; "Eugene wounded? And wounded by your hand, Ottokar? A boy, a poor harmless boy? Oh! impossible! This is some egregious mistake, and..."

"No, lady; there is no mistake in this; the peasants told the truth. It was my hand, which struck Eugene to the ground; for Eugene was the wretch who (as I before mentioned to you) attempted this evening the precious life of Blanche."

"You rave, Sir Ottokar! Eugene, an assassin? The assassin of a female, too? He, who bears to the very name of woman a love, a reverence almost idolatrous? He, the gentlest, tenderest..."

"Lady, I saw him myself; I heard the shrieks of Blanche with my own ears! I saw her sink at his feet in terror; I saw Eugene with his sword drawn on the very point of plunging it in her bosom..."

"Nay, nay! Let us not waste our time in disputing about Eugene. Be he innocent, or be he guilty, your hands are stained with his blood, and here you are no longer in safety. So dear as Eugene is to my husband..."

"Surely, Countess, surely, he will be no longer dear to him, when Rudiger learns his guilt; or if he still protects him, that protection will prove, that Rudiger himself cannot be innocent. Criminal as Eugene is, if he can still inspire his master with any sentiment, but indignation, but hatred..."

"Hatred? His master? Oh! Ottokar, you know not... there is a mystery about that boy...there is a secret reason... Rudiger hate Eugene? Eugene, who is his own... I mean... I would say... Eugene, whom Rudiger loves as dearly, as if he were his own son!"

The eagerness with which she endeavored to recall her words; the hesitation with which she pronounced the correcting phrase; the color which crimsoned her cheeks at having so nearly divulged her husband's secret; all these immediately dispelled the cloud which overhung the birth of Eugene. Ottokar instantly comprehended how dear an interest Rudiger took in the page's welfare, and how odious the man must appear in his eyes who had plunged his sword in the boy's bosom. He hesitated, what course to pursue; Magdalena advised his leaving her to reconcile the mind of her husband to what had happened, and not to repeat his visit at the castle, till she should inform him, that his present offense was forgotten and forgiven; and the knight was on the point of following her counsels when the door was again thrown open, and the Count of Frankheim re-entered the room.

The Countess shuddered, as she cast an anxious glance upon his countenance. His face was of a deadly paleness; the deepest gloom sat upon his frowning brows; his burning eyes glared with terrible expression: yet a smile of forced urbanity played round his bloodless lips, and on his entrance he bowed his proud head toward Ottokar with an air of unusual condescension.

"You are welcome, sir knight!" said he. "This visit affords me a satisfaction totally unexpected. Magdalena, your nephew will need some refreshment; will you not see that it is prepared?"

The tone in which this question was asked converted it into a command; she was obliged to obey, and could only whisper to Ottokar in passing—"Be on your guard, for God's sake!"

"Be seated, Sir Ottokar," resumed the Count. "Nay, no ceremony! And now may I inquire, what lucky circumstance brings you hither? It is not often, that Frankheim Castle is honored by your presence. You come, I understand, from Orrenberg; you are a friend of Gustavus, and a suitor of his daughter; is it not so? A fair lady and an excellent choice; I am told that her influence over you is unbounded; that what she desires, be it right, or be it wrong, you perform with all the ardor of a true lover; and in truth, it is fitting that you should. But as I said before, you come straight from Orrenberg; perhaps, you bring some message from your friend Gustavus? Some conciliatory proposal... some explanation of past circumstances... or perhaps, he has sent me a defiance in return for mine, and your friendship for him induces you to appear before me in the sacred character of his herald. Am I right, Sir Ottokar?"

"As the herald of Gustavus? No, Count Rudiger: I come here as your friend, if you will permit me to be so; as your guest, unless you have forsworn the rights of hospitality."

"My guest? Oh! undoubtedly! You do me but too much honor! But... am I to understand, then, that you bring no commission from Orrenberg?"

"Yes; one which I trust will convince you that I am not more the friend of Orrenberg than of Frankheim. Count, Gustavus wishes to hold with you a personal conference."

"A conference? With me?"

"You may well be surprised; I was so myself when he first mentioned it; but he asserts with such solemn adjurations his innocence..."

"His innocence? Indeed?"

"He declares himself so certain of proving to your complete satisfaction that he had no hand in Joscelyn's murder, and he is so anxious of laying before you a plan for putting an end to all feuds in a manner equally beneficial and agreeable to both families, that if you will but listen to him."

"Listen to him? Oh! by all means. When you see him again, pray, assure him that an interview with him will give me the highest satisfaction."

"When I see him? Dear Count, since you charge me with so welcome a commission, I will hasten back to Orrenberg without a moment's delay. Oh! From what a weight shall I relieve his mind, and how wisely do you act in showing this readiness to conciliation! Rudiger, may the right hand, which I thus stretch toward Heaven, wither and rot away if I am perjured in swearing that I believe Gustavus to be innocent. Now then, farewell! Yet hold! there are two points...two unlucky accidents, which have lately happened... and which while unexplained... must have produced a disadvantageous impression upon your mind, and may be the source of future dissension. Permit me therefore to mention, that Eugene..."

"I know it; I have heard it already. Eugene has been mortally wounded in the neighborhood of Orrenberg Castle. You need say no more about it."

"Not mortally, Count. I am assured, that his wounds are not mortal; I trust that he will recover."

"Not mortal, you say? Nay, just as you please!"

"Count Rudiger!"

"Anything more? You mentioned two accidents, I think, and..."

"Before I enter upon the second, permit me to explain that if there was any fault in the first, it proceeded entirely from the conduct of Eugene himself. He attempted to assassinate the Lady Blanche this evening, and..."

"Oh! to be sure! Extremely probable, and extremely wrong; the boy deserved his fate! And I make no doubt that Gustavus supposes him to have been instigated by me to commit this crime? Nay, I confess, that seems highly probable too!"

"No, Rudiger, you wrong him. It is true, everyone else at Orrenberg accuses you, but Gustavus himself loudly asserts his conviction of your innocence."

"Fiend! fiend! Oh! artful devil... ten thousand pardons, Baron! A sudden pain... but 'tis gone; I am quite myself again. Now then; the second little accident...?"

"The herald whom you sent to Orrenberg two days ago was knocked on the head; they told me so before; but of course, Gustavus had no hand in the affair!"

"He had none, indeed. I was present myself and witnessed his exertions to calm the fury of the mob; till unluckily, exhausted with fatigue, and overcome with apprehension, he fainted, and while he was insensible..."

"He fainted? That was unlucky indeed!"

"This misfortune has distressed Gustavus beyond measure; he has commissioned me to say that any reparation which you can demand in honor..."

"Reparation for such a trifle? Oh! absurd! The thing is really not worth talking of."

"Count of Frankheim!"

"For after all, the man was but a herald; and what is a herald, you know!"

"What is he? Permit me to say..."

"How is this, Sir Ottokar? You espouse the cause of heralds so warmly that one would think you were a herald yourself; and in fact you are so! You bring the Count of Orrenberg's messages; you make the Count of Orrenberg's conciliatory proposals; and therefore to all intents and purposes you are the Count of Orrenberg's herald. Is it not so, sir knight?"

"Rudiger, I repeat it, I am here only as your friend, and as the Lady Magdalena's near kinsman—and even should the laws of chivalry not induce you to respect the herald, the rights of hospitality must surely make you consider the person of your guest as sacred."

"Sacred? My guest? Oh! Undoubtedly! Nothing can be better said, or more certain—the person of my guest must always be considered as sacred by me; only... there is one trilling point, of which it may be as well to make you aware.—I also am very subject to fainting."

"Indeed?" exclaimed Ottokar, starting; then fixing his eyes on those of Rudiger, he read in them an expression which almost froze the marrow in his bones—"Farewell, Count Rudiger!" said he, and hastily quitted the room.

The Count remained in his seat, reclining his head upon his hand, silent, motionless, and gloomy. Some minutes elapsed, and still he moved not.

"Save him! Save him!" shrieked Magdalena, as she rushed into the chamber, pale as death; "hasten to his rescue, Rudiger! For God's sake, hasten! Look! Look"—and she threw open the window which commanded the courtyard, and from whence the light of the full moon and the blaze of numerous torches permitted her to observe distinctly what was passing below. "He is surrounded... Ottokar... the people, the whole crowd of them, with swords, with clubs...fly, fly, Rudiger, and rescue him!—Merciful Heaven! They drag him from his horse... they throw him on the earth... they will kill him! They will murder him!—Nay, look yourself!"

"Come to the window; speak to the wild rabble, or their fury... Ha! he forces himself out of their clutches! He draws his sword... he fights... he drives them back... now, now, my lord! Now they can hear you! Seize this interval of fear, and command them... Alas! alas! Now they all rush upon him at once, like madmen; he defends himself still, but their numbers..."

"Rudiger! Rudiger! For mercy's sake, for God's sake, call to them from the window... speak one word, speak but one word, and... Ah! his head... a blow... he staggers... and now another... and another... it's done! it's done!—He falls! He is dead!—Oh! Blessed Mary, receive his soul to mercy!"

She sank upon her knees, pressed to her lips the golden cross, which hung at her bosom, and passed some minutes in fervent supplication for the sins of her unhappy nephew. As she prayed, the excess of horror gradually abated; religion already poured balm into her still bleeding wounds; the thought of eternal happiness hereafter, enabled her to sustain the weight of her present afflictions; the agony of grief was softened into melancholy tenderness; she found, that she could again breathe freely; and a torrent of grateful tears rushed into her burning eyes and relieved the burden of her overcharged bosom.

She rose from her knees; she turned toward her husband, who still sat motionless in his chair.

"Rudiger!" she said, "your guest, your kinsman has been murdered in your castle, almost before your eyes; it would have cost you but one word, but one look, nay, the very sight of their lord's countenance, his mere presence would have been sufficient to recall the rabble to their duty, and terrify them from accomplishing their barbarous purpose! I told you what would happen; I called you; I implored you; and still you were deaf to my cries; and still you moved not! Oh! what cruel insensibility! Oh! what inhuman obstinacy! Now God grant that in that bitter hour when you most want his help, he may not be as slow to afford it as you have been to the wretched Ottokar!"

The Count replied not. The door opened, and Wilfred entered.

"Noble lord!" said he, "your orders are obeyed."

"Obeyed? His orders?" repeated Magdalena with a shriek of surprise and horror. She fixed her eyes upon the countenance of her husband with a look of dreadful inquiry. Every muscle in his gigantic form seemed convulsed by some horrible sensation; the deepest gloom darkened every feature; the wind from the unclosed window agitated his raven locks, and every hair appeared to writhe itself. His eyeballs glared; his teeth chattered; his lips trembled; and yet a smile of satisfied vengeance played horribly round them. His complexion appeared suddenly to be changed to the dark tincture of an African; the expression of his countenance was dreadful, was diabolical. Magdalena, as she gazed upon his face, thought that she gazed upon the face of a demon.

"Obeyed?" After a long pause she repeated once more, "Rudiger! Obeyed!"—He raised his eyes to hers, but he could not support their gaze. He turned hastily away, and concealed his countenance with his robe.

"Now then," she resumed, "the whole is clear! Fool that I was! And I called you to the innocent youth's rescue! Fye, oh! fye!—This is not the action of a warrior, of a man! This is so odious, so despicable, that I, your wife, your fond, your humble, your much-injured, your ever-enduring wife, even I pronounce it odious and despicable, and dare to proclaim aloud my hatred and my contempt. Oh! shame! shame!—How the man sits there, and must endure to hear the just reproaches of one whom he knows so inferior in all things but virtue; of a woman, weak in mind, weak in body, but strong in conscious innocence, and therefore stronger than himself! Heaven can witness with what truth, with what fondness, with what adoration, I have ever loved you, Rudiger; but the feeling of what is right is superior to all other feelings; but the voice of justice will be heard; and not even the husband of my heart, not even the father of my children is to me a character so sacred as to stifle the sentence of my reason, of my conscience, which cries to me aloud 'The husband of your heart, the father of your children, is a murderer!' Your caprice, your pride, your wayward humors, your infidelities, I have borne them all, and loved you still; but when I see your hands stained with the blood of your kinsman, of your guest, of a man who came hither solely for your service, who had sacrificed to your welfare all his heart's dearest wishes; when I see your hands stained with his blood, with his innocent blood... Oh! Rudiger! Rudiger! is it possible that I should ever love you more!"

Her heart agonized, her brain almost distracted, she fled from her husband's presence, and inclosing herself within her oratory, passed the night in prayer equally for the souls of the murdered one and of his unhappy murderer!

CHAPTER VIII

—"Semina, floresque, et succos incoquit acres;
Addit et exceptas lund pernocte pruinas.
Et strigis in fames ipsis cum carnibus alas.
Vivacisque jecur cervi; quibus insuper addit
Ora caputque novem cornicis sacula passæ."—
Ovid.
—"Here boil'd she many a seed, and herb, and flower.
And dews in moonshine culled at midnight hour.
Bat's wings, a stag's still-panting heart, and last
A raven's head, o'er which nine hundred years had past."—

While his father was thus plunging himself in an abyss of real guilt, Osbright was hastening in eager pursuit of means to elucidate the imaginary crime of Gustavus. The forest was thick; the way was long, and difficult to find without a guide. Osbright had obtained ample instructions respecting the course which he was to hold, and he believed it impossible to make a mistake; but his mind occupied with canvassing the obstacles, which impeded his union with Blanche and the reconciliation of the families, and in weighing the arguments for and against success in his present pursuit, he suffered himself to fall into a reverie, during which his steed directed his course entirely at his own pleasure. At length the animal thought proper to stop. The cessation of motion recalled Osbright to himself; he looked around and found himself in the deepest part of the wood and where no beaten path was discernible.

Which way to guide his horse he had not the most distant idea. Highly incensed at his own negligence, he urged his courser on at random, being only able to decide that to remain where he was then was the worst thing that he could do; whereas by proceeding he might possibly either regain the proper road, or might find some peasant to direct him how to find it. He therefore continued to hasten onward, till his horse put his foot into a pit-fall, and entangled himself too completely to be extricated by any efforts of his rider.

Osbright was now at a complete loss, what to do. The groans of the animal announced that he had received some injury, though the thickness of the boughs excluding all assistance from the moon, the knight was unable to ascertain the nature of his hurt. A sound, like distant thunder, seemed to foretell a coming storm, and to remind him that it was probable in a short time that his situation would become still more disagreeable; while his meditations on the means of extricating himself from his present embarrassment received very unpleasant interruptions from the howling of wolves and other wild beasts by whom the forest was infested. Suddenly Osbright fancied that he saw something glimmer among the trees. He hastily hewed away with his sword some of the intervening branches, which impeded his view, and was delighted to perceive the light of a fire, which evidently shed its rays through the casement of a cottage-window at no great distance. Thither he resolved to hasten, and request its owners to assist him in recovering his horse.

He arrived at the spot, whence the light proceeded. Here stood a low and wretched-looking hut, rudely constructed, and covered with fern and withered boughs. Before he gave notice of his presence, the youth judged it prudent to ascertain the nature of the inhabitants. Accordingly he approached the small window without noise, whence he had a perfect view into the hut's interior..A young girl, who seemed to be about fifteen, and whose patched garments declared her to be the child of poverty, sat upon a low stool by the hearth. Sometimes she fed the fire with dry sticks, and at others she cast different materials into an iron kettle, which was boiling before her.

She frequently stirred its contents and seemed extremely intent upon her occupation. Osbright doubted not that she was preparing the repast of her parents, or perhaps of her master, and he was on the point of lifting the latch of the door, when he heard the girl speak, as if addressing someone in an adjoining room.

"Yes! yes!" said she; "I hear you; all is going on well!" And then turning again to the cauldron, "Now then," she continued; "once again! First for father.

"Peace to his bones! May they sleep in the cell, Ne'er mingled for mischief in poison, nor spell!"

"Rest in the coffin! All ghastly and pale, By night may his ghost never wander and wail!"

"Joy to the soul! May he rise without fears, When the trumpet, to sinners so dreadful, he hears."

"Now for my grandmother.

"Feuds with the Fiends! May the Hag's evil eye Ne'er cause..."

"Barbara! Barbara!" screamed a cracked voice, from the inner room. "Idle hussy, what are you thinking about? I'm sure, you're not repeating the three wishes!"

"Sure, are you? Nay, for certain, if the saints are half as deaf as you are, I repeat them to little purpose. Set your heart at rest, I tell you; I warrant you, all goes right.

"Joy to the soul! May he rise..."

"No, no! I said that; where was I? Stay! Oh! Aye, now I remember."

"Feuds with the Fiends! May the Hag's evil eye Ne'er cause our cow Brindle to droop and to die!"

"Mercy to man! May her limbs cease to ache, Which the ague now forces to shiver and shake!"

Safety with Saints! Let not Satan succeed In laming her tongue, when she's saying her creed!"

"And now for myself!"

"Holy and sweet! May the knot soon be tied By the priest, which shall make me some honest man's bride!"

"Sorrow and Joy! When in childbirth I lie, Light be my labor, and..."
Here her eye fell upon Osbright, who, having lifted up the latch of
the door softly, had entered, and was now standing beside her. "Oh!
preserve me, all blessed saints and angels!" cried the girl with a loud
shriek, and sprang from her seat. "Mercy upon me, sir knight; who
are you, and what brings you here?"

"Be not alarmed, my pretty lass!" answered Osbright. "My horse has
fallen into a pit-fall, and I need assistance to draw him out. Are there
any men belonging to this cottage, who..."

"Oh! no, sir knight; there is no one here, but myself and my old
grandmother, who is confined to her bed with a terrible ague-fit! But
to the right, you will find a narrow path which leads to the village of
Orrenberg; there you may procure assistance in plenty; it is not
above a mile off; and now, good sir knight, be gone, I entreat you!" —
And she turned again to the hearth.

"To the right, I think, you said?" inquired the youth. "My good girl,
leave your cookery to itself for a few minutes, and just point out the
path of which you spoke, and an ample reward. . ."

"Oh! no, no, no! I could not stir a step out of this room for the
universe, sir knight! So, pry'thee, interrupt me no longer, or you'll
certainly... look you there now!" she exclaimed, running to the
cauldron, and beginning to stir it again with great eagerness. "I
thought what would come of talking to me! The brewage was just
going to boil over, and then all the charm would have been to do
over again!"

"The charm?"

"No, no! Not a charm! I did not mean to say charm... . I don't know
what I meant to say; but I know, I wish, that you would not interrupt
me any longer. Now do go away, there's a good young knight; now
go!" — And she began again to mutter her rhymes.

"Barbara!" called again the cracked voice from the inner room. "For Heaven's love, don't forget the ague!"

"No, no!" replied Barbara, "nor the cow either."

"Did I tell you," resumed the voice, "did I tell you, that the snail-shells must be whole? If they are cracked in the least part, the broth will be spoiled, and then the child's finger will have no power or virtue."

"A child's finger?" Osbright started, and his heart beat violently at the sound. He recollected that Father Peter had mentioned the loss of Joscelyn's little finger of the right hand.

Should this prove to be the same, here was a clue furnished which might lead to the most important discoveries! While he made this reflection, Barbara answered her grandmother that she had observed her caution respecting the shells, and bade her make herself quite easy.

"Good! good!" said again the old woman. "Only be sure that you put in cobwebs enough, for that is a prime ingredient." — And now Barbara resumed her entreaties that the stranger would leave the cottage.

"By no means!" answered he resolutely, "there seems to be something improper going on here. A child's finger is boiling in that cauldron, and I must know for what purpose you procured it, and in what manner you came by it, before I stir one step from this apartment."

"Now indeed, sir knight!" cried the girl evidently alarmed, "the purpose for which it is intended is a very harmless one. A child's finger is boiling yonder, I must confess; but it is only to make a spell of great virtue, though so innocent that the Virgin herself need not have scrupled to make use of it. The kettle contains the broth of good-luck, and whatever wishes I pronounce, while it is making, sooner or later will all come to pass. And then when it is done, the child's finger being passed nine times through a wedding-ring, it affords an infallible cure for the ague and the earache; and being wrapped in the skin of a dormouse with a sprig of St. John's wort, and laid under the threshold of the door, it is better than an old horseshoe, and neither witch nor devil will venture to put their noses over it; and being dipped in bat's blood, and well rubbed in...but mercy on me, what am I about? I ought to be alone while the broth is brewing, for my grandmother herself must not set her foot in the room, because she's not a virgin. Now, dear, good young knight, go along, for if any impure person is present, the charm is quite spoiled."

"Very possibly," observed Osbright; "but though an impure person may do so much mischief, the presence of another pure person ought to make the work go on still better."

"Indeed? Why, as to that point, my grandmother gave no instructions, and it may very well be, as you say, sir knight! Stay a moment, and I'll ask her."

"By no means!" resumed Osbright, detaining her with a look of feigned severity. "It would be quite superfluous, as I am determined not only to remain where I am, but to know by what means the child's finger came into your possession."

"Oh! Gracious! Sir knight! My grandmother charged me not to say a word about the finger to any soul breathing. She said that it might bring us into much trouble, in spite of our innocence."

"It will bring you into much more trouble, if you do not obey me without a moment's hesitation; for I shall hasten to the next village and depose that I found you in the very act of composing an unlawful potion. Both yourself and your grandmother will be seized as witches, and..."

"Oh! all ye blessed saints protect us!" cried the girl trembling in every limb. "That is exactly what we are afraid of; that is it which has obliged us to take refuge in this wild forest out of the reach of every human eye. Indeed, sir knight, we are honest creatures; but my grandmother is a wise woman and knows a power of strange secrets and all the hidden virtues of herbs and plants; and so some ignorant evil-minded person accused her of dealing in sorcery, and if she had not escaped in time, the poor innocent woman would most probably have been burnt for a witch, only because she knew a little more than her neighbors. Now, good sir knight, do not depose against us; only promise to keep our secret, and you shall know every syllable of the matter as faithfully, as if I was kneeling at confession before the Father-Abbot of St. John's himself!"

Osbright gave the required promise—and now he listened with interest, which almost deprived him of the power of breathing, while the girl related that a fortnight had scarcely elapsed, since she found in the wood a young boy, apparently not above nine years old, and at the point of death. She endeavored to save his life but in vain; he had only time to tell her that while separated from his friends during the chase, he had been seized by a wolf; that he had drawn his little dagger and had defended himself so successfully, that though in the contest he gave himself several wounds with his own weapon, he achieved the death of the ferocious animal; but before he could accomplish this, his bosom was dreadfully lacerated, and he had lost so much blood before the girl's arrival, that in spite of-all her efforts to succor him, he soon breathed his last.

Assured that he was quite dead, she left the fatal spot but took with her the dead wolf, whose skin, she knew, would be an acceptable winter-gift to her grandmother. The old woman, however, on hearing the story, informed her that she had left something behind much more valuable than the skins of all the wolves in the forest. This was the little finger of the child's left hand, which, being boiled with certain mystical ingredients, possessed a thousand important and beneficial properties. Barbara greatly regretted her not having been aware of its virtue; especially as she had taken notice, that in struggling with the wolf the boy had broken that identical finger, and as it seemed only to hang by the skin, nothing would have been more easy for her than to make herself mistress of it. However, it might possibly not be too late, and she hurried back to the scene of death. The corpse was still lying there; no one observed her, and she secured the finger; but in one minute more she would have been too late. She heard footsteps approaching, and had scarcely time to conceal herself behind a bush, when a man arrived at the place whom she well knew to be a domestic of the Count of Orrenberg, having frequently seen him at the castle, when she occasionally ventured thither to dispose of the eggs of her poultry and the milk of the aforesaid cow Brindle. The man, she said, seemed to be greatly distressed and shocked at finding the poor child weltering in his blood; he lifted him in his arms, and she watched him to the river's side, where she left him bathing the child's forehead, washing the blood from the wounds, and using all those efforts to recover him, which, experience had already assured her, must be ineffectual. However, she judged it unwise to tell him so, lest seeing her clothes stained with the blood which had trickled from the dead wolf, and perhaps missing the little finger from the child's hand, he might be induced to suspect her of having been accessory to his death. She thereupon left him still engaged in his charitable endeavors, and returned to her grandmother with her important prize; the use of which, however, had been deferred till the present evening, on account of the difficulty of collecting the other ingredients of the charm.

Such was Barbara's narrative, and Osbright heard with rapture the confirmation of Gustavus's innocence. He asked the girl why she had not disclosed these circumstances when inquiry was made respecting the child's supposed murder; but no such inquiry had reached this secluded hut, whose existence was unknown even at Orrenberg, though so near, and whose inhabitants had no intercourse with the rest of the world, except when necessity compelled Barbara to venture with fear and trembling, either to the castle to dispose of her ware or to the village to purchase those few articles of life which were indispensable.

Osbright rewarded the girl's information liberally, and then having received certain instructions for reaching the neighboring village, he set forward to request assistance for his embarrassed horse. His plans were now changed; and instead of prosecuting his journey, he determined to hasten to Sir Lennard of Kleeborn with the explanation of those circumstances which (as the warrior had assured him) formed the principal objection to his union with Blanche and to a reconciliation between the hostile kinsmen.

CHAPTER IX

"To you my soul's affections move.
Devoutly, warmly true;
My life has been a task of love.
One long, long thought of you."
T. Moore.

Osbright found the castle of Kleeborn in all the hurry of warlike preparation. The courtyard was strewn with swords and lances; on every side vassals were seen employed in furbishing up their shields and breastplates, and from every quarter resounded the noise of the busy armorers. The youth was too eager to impart the purport of his visit to Sir Lennard to allow himself time for inquiring the cause of all this bustle. He hastened to his friend's apartment, and started back in surprise and disappointment at the marked coldness with which he was received.

With all the frankness and impetuosity of his age, he demanded the reason of this altered treatment; and he now learned, with equal grief and horror the crime with which his father had burdened his soul, and the effect which it had produced at Oirenberg. Sir Ottokar had always been particularly acceptable to Gustavus and his wife; his deference to their opinions, and the partial interest which he had ever taken in their concerns, had not only flattered their pride, but had even been of essential benefit on many most important occasions. His wealth, his power, his high birth and military talents rendered his friendship and support a treasure to those on whom it was conferred; his evident adoration of Blanche had made them for some time past consider him as their future son; and the generosity, with which in their last interview he had sacrificed his own pretensions to the wishes of Blanche and the welfare of her family, had exalted their esteem to a pitch of the highest admiration; a sentiment which was shared by Sir Lennard, whose heart Ottokar's disinterested conduct had completely won. When, therefore, the news of his murder reached Orrenberg, the consternation, the astonishment, the grief, the thirst for revenge, and the bursts of frantic anger, which it excited, exceeded all powers of description. Ulrica poured forth without restraint the effusions of all that jealousy and mistrust which she had so long stifled within her bosom against the house of Frankheim. The gentle Blanche wept floods of tears, alternately pitying the kind youth, who from her childhood had been to her as a brother, and bewailing this fresh obstacle to a reconciliation with her lover's family; while Gustavus now mourned the loss of his friend, whom he considered as having fallen a victim to the warmth with which he had espoused the interests of Orrenberg, now expatiated on his numerous merits and his own extensive obligations to him, and now vowed to enact a dreadful vengeance for his death on the barbarous bloody Rudiger. Sir Lennard, inspired with similar indignation, agreed that no vengeance could be exacted too severe for such a crime; he promised to assist Gustavus in obtaining it with his whole power; and having sworn to renounce all intercourse with the house of Frankheim, he hastened to his own castle to arm his vassals, and lead them to the assistance of Gustavus.

Osbright listened in the utmost consternation, while the above circumstances were narrated by his host; but the vehemence with which he reprobated Ottokar's murder and the agony which he evidently felt at hearing the guilt of his father were such as speedily to remove from Sir Lennard's mind every unfavorable impression respecting the youth himself. The good knight, therefore, gave him his hand with his accustomed cordiality, and assured him of his undiminished anxiety for his welfare. Heartily did he wish his future happiness; but he added that after his solemn promise to Gustavus, he must confine himself to merely wishing it. Osbright must now prosecute his love-suit entirely by his own address; if he could obtain the lady, no one would feel more joy at his success than Sir Lennard. But never more should the name of Osbright be pronounced by him at the castle of Orrenberg; he had sworn it, and nothing could induce him to violate his oath.

Entreaties, that he would change this resolution, proved unavailing, and Osbright departed with a heavy heart. Yet a hint which had fallen from Sir Lennard had not been wasted in the air.

Could Blanche be induced to fly with him and unite her fate to his, the Castle of Kleeborn would afford them a secure refuge during the first storm of paternal indignation. He was himself innocent of any offense, and doubtless Gustavus would soon forbear to confound the son with the father. The irrevocable knot once tied, the two families must needs reconcile themselves to a measure which could no longer be avoided. Time, the great healer of wounds, might even obliterate the remembrance of this atrocious act from the minds of the different parties; and their respective interests being inseparably blended by this marriage, Mistrust (that odious and malignant monster, which for so long had blasted the happiness of the hostile kinsmen) must needs perish for want of aliment. That Blanche could be persuaded to abandon those parents, whom she loved so passionately, Osbright with justice greatly doubted; but he resolved that at least the attempt should be made. An interview with her must be immediately procured; then if she refused to share his fate, he determined to bid an eternal adieu both to Blanche and to Germany, to join the Crusaders who were on the point of departing on their holy mission, and to lose on the ensanguined plains of Palestine at once his sorrows, his affection, and his life.

But how was he to obtain this interview? Blanche was not to visit the grotto till informed of his return by Sir Lennard, and Sir Lennard had positively refused to interfere any further in the business. He in vain looked round for some other friend to render him this service; and after much deliberation, be determined that under pretense of disposing of her ware at the castle, the young Barbara might easily deliver a letter to Blanche. He, therefore, hastened once more to the cottage in the wood. His liberality soon induced the girl to undertake the commission. Writing materials were procured at the next village; and Barbara soon departed with a most pressing letter, for the answer to which he determined to wait at the cottage.

But Blanche was no longer mistress of her actions. In the height of their indignation at Ottokar's murder, her parents had insisted upon her renouncing all thoughts of a union with Osbright of Frankheim. Her heart would not allow her to make this renunciation. She protested against the injustice of implicating the son in the father's guilt and avowed the impossibility of withdrawing her affection. Ulrica, whose passions were violent and whose understanding was not strong, was highly indignant at her daughter's disobedience, declared that she would see her no more till she was awakened to a proper sense of duty, and order her to be confined to her own apartment; as to Gustavus, though he disapproved in his heart of such compulsory measures, yet having entirely given up the management of Blanche to his wife hitherto, he forbore on this occasion also to interfere with her orders.

Willingly would the poor Blanche have complied with her lover's request for a last parting interview, to which he had confined himself in his letter; thinking the plan of elopement more likely to be adopted by her if presented without allowing her time for consideration; but how was that compliance to be effected? She was a captive, and could not even leave her own apartment, much less the castle. In this dilemma she resolved to appeal to her nurse, the only person who had access to her, and one who had ever showed toward her the affection of a mother.

The good woman at first remonstrated loudly against the impropriety of her lady's quitting her father's home clandestinely, and insisted upon the danger of her being encountered by the emissaries of the Count of Frankheim, from whose bloody designs she had so lately and so narrowly escaped. But the prayers and tears of Blanche conquered all resistance; and on her promising to be absent but a single hour and to wear such a disguise as must effectually prevent her being recognized either by friend or foe, Margaret consented to assist her temporary evasion.

Her son, a young peasant, was at that time on a visit to her and resident in the castle. His stature was nearly the same as that of Blanche; it was accordingly agreed, that Margaret should procure permission for him to take leave of his young mistress, who was also his foster sister, previous to his quitting the castle; that Blanche arrayed in a suit of his clothes might easily elude the vigilance of her guards, while he remained concealed in her apartment till her return; for which his being supposed to have remembered something of importance to say to his mother would afford a plausible reason; and that, as the late occurrences had occasioned the private passage to be shut up, Barbara should wait near the drawbridge to conduct Blanche to the grotto by a path through the woods, by which means she would be less exposed to observation and discovery than if obliged to traverse the usual and beaten road. Blanche adopted this plan with eagerness, and rewarded her kind nurse for her invention with a thousand benedictions and caresses; but as this discussion had lasted till the approach of night, it was agreed to defer the interview till the succeeding evening..This being arranged, Barbara hastened back to the cottage with a letter whose assurances of undiminished affection filled the heart of Osbright with hope, joy, and gratitude. To prevent by his presence even the possibility of danger, he engaged to meet Barbara near the drawbridge at the appointed hour; and he now sought the villager, to whose care he had intrusted his wounded horse, and from whom he had borrowed a sorry beast for his excursion to the Castle of Kleeborn.

He found his courser perfectly recovered, rewarded the villager for his attention, and he now resolved to return to Frankheim; where his plans made it necessary for him to furnish himself with gold and jewels for the expenses of his journey in case of his departure for the Holy Land, or for the sustenance of his wife in case he should be so fortunate as to prevail on Blanche to accompany him in his proposed flight. His course was again directed to St. John's Chapel; where the intelligence communicated by Brother Peter, respecting Ottokar's murder, Eugene's illness, and the state of Castle Frankheim, confirmed him in the prudence of his determinations. He found that under the present circumstances there was no hope of getting his father to countenance his affection for the daughter of Gustavus; but his knowledge of Magdalena's character and of the warm undeviating affection she had ever borne him convinced him that he ran no danger of her betraying him should he venture to confess to her his love and his designs; and that if they were once made known to her, she would assist his wishes to the very utmost of her power. Accordingly, he requested Brother Peter to convey a letter to the Countess, which must be delivered with the greatest secrecy into her own hands; in this, he disclosed to her his irrevocable vows to

Blanche, entreated her to use every means to soften his father's heart toward the family of Orrenberg, and finally requested her to transmit to him by the bearer a casket containing gold and some jewels of value, which she would find in a particular part of his bed chamber.

The good friar, though still ignorant of the name of his young guest, already was too much fascinated by his manners and conversation to refuse him any honest service; accordingly, without requiring to have his curiosity gratified by an explanation of its nature, he readily accepted the commission, and departed with the letter for the Castle of Frankheim.

CHAPTER X

"Horror and doubt distract
His troubled thoughts, and in his bosom stir
The hell within him—Now conscience wakes despair
Which slumbered; wakes the better memory
Of what he was, what is, and what must be.
Worse; of worse deeds, worse sufferings must ensue."
Milton.

Anger had satiated itself with blood; the tempest was past; the voice of conscience now could be heard again, and dreadful was its sound in the ears of the guilty Rudiger. Blinded by passion, he had persuaded himself that in putting Ottokar to death he had exercised a just retaliation for the murder of his herald; but now that the illusion was dissipated, he shuddered at perceiving that the two actions wore a very different complexion. Gustavus at least had given no positive orders for the one; but no such excuse could be alleged for the other: the one at least was sudden, and might have occurred through accident; the other was premeditated, and could only have happened through design; again, the herald was the partisan of a foe, and was indeed a foe himself; but Ottokar was a friend, was a kinsman, was a guest who had trusted to the laws of knightly hospitality and knightly honor—laws which had been found insufficient to preserve his life Conscience and his wife's reproaches had awakened Rudiger to a full sense of his guilt; but instead of being beneficial, fatally dreadful were the effect which this conviction produced upon his character. He was not a villain; on the contrary, crimes filled his soul with horror and indignation; nay, he possessed a thousand noble, generous, and heroic feelings; but he was the slave of tempestuous passions, and even in the most laudable movements of his nature, he might rather be said to detest vice than to love virtue.

Now then, when he saw himself on a sudden the object of his own abhorrence, of that abhorrence which he had formerly expressed so loudly and so warmly against others; when he heard the bitter reproaches of Magdalena, and felt in all the agony of his soul, that her reproaches were deserved; he sank at once into the deepest gloom of despondency, into all the horrors of self-loathing, and all the bitterness of mental misery. He indulged no wish of reparation; he formed no plan of repentance; he sought no excuse for his crime; he rather exaggerated its atrocity. What he now felt toward Gustavus was no longer suspicion, or jealousy, or ill-will!

No—it was the deepest, deadliest hatred; it was a burning thirst for vengeance, which the blood of the whole family of Orrenberg seemed scarcely enough to quench. He was guilty, he was the most execrable of mortals, he was odious in his own eyes; and what punishment could be inflicted too severe on the man, who had made him so? That man was Gustavus; on Gustavus he swore to be revenged with the most dreadful imprecations; the magnitude of this one crime made him consider all future ones as but of little account, and he became the more a villain from his very abhorrence of vice.

When the first emotions of grief and horror had subsided, and Magdalena's heart no longer prevented her better judgment from exercising its influence, she regretted bitterly her having exposed her feelings so plainly before her lord. She was well aware that with his temper reproaches could only serve to exasperate his passions, and unqualified opposition to confirm him in a course of error. With the dawn of morning, therefore, she hastened to his chamber, determined to remove as much as possible the impression which she had left on his mind at their last parting. She wished to soothe the agonies of his bleeding conscience, to convince him gently and gradually that all these mischiefs arose from the long-subsisting and unnatural enmity of the two houses, and (if possible) by using the gentlest persuasion to win from him a consent that the occurrence of similar disasters should be prevented by the union of Blanche and Osbright, and consequently of the dearest interests of the two families. But her good intentions were frustrated; she was refused admittance to Rudiger, who passed the next four-and twenty hours in the solitude of his chamber, alternately execrating himself and others, and passing by turns from the depth of the blackest gloom to the extreme of the wildest fury.

No one but Wilfred was suffered to approach him; nor would he quit his chamber, till informed of the arrival of Eugene, whom (though his wound was not mortal) it had been at first judged imprudent to remove from the monastery of St. John. Though he had hitherto endeavored to conceal it even from himself, partly through prudence, partly through pride, it was in truth this unacknowledged boy who possessed the whole paternal love of Rudiger. The difference of his sensations toward him and Osbright partook of those which he had felt toward their respective mothers. His esteem, his admiration were bestowed in the highest degree on Magdalena; but his heart had never melted with love but for the unhappy Agatha. Osbright was his heir, was a hero; he was fond of him, but on Eugene he doted. In the one, he prized the transmitter of his name, which was so precious to his vanity; but he cherished Eugene for his own sake. It is true, if he had been asked—"which of the youths should perish"—he would have sacrificed Eugene without a moment's hesitation; for, in the bosom of Rudiger pride ever bore a sway far superior to that of tenderness; but had he been asked—"which of them he could consent never to see again"—he would have felt as little doubt in answering—"Osbright"—nor perhaps would have felt very deeply the deprivation, though the being his heir was the strongest claim to his attention. Still the reflection, that he must be his heir, made Rudiger entertain some little jealousy toward him; and in the presence of Osbright, the father's self-love felt painfully wounded by being sensible, that the perfection of his son made the defects of his own character appear in a more glaring light. On the other hand he saw in Eugene a poor defenseless being, whom he had brought into a world of sorrow, where his lot was hard, and against whose difficulties he was ill calculated to struggle. He pitied him for his destitute situation, and he loved him for his likeness to his wretched mother. In short, Eugene was dearer to him than Osbright; but the pride of blood was a thousand times dearer to him than either: he would have sacrificed his own life to preserve Eugene's; but he would have sacrificed Eugene's as well as his own to preserve in Osbright "the future Count of Frankheim."

No sooner was he informed of the youth's arrival, than he hastened to visit him; but he had scarcely passed the threshold of his chamber, when Magdalena stood before him. He started back, and a deep gloom darkened all his features. In vain did she address him in the most soothing language, and endeavor to extenuate the atrocity of Ottokar's murder; he listened in silence, and only replied by a look of scornful incredulity. In vain did she recant the too hasty declaration of her sentiments toward him, and assure him of her undiminished affection; the bending of his head with constrained politeness and a smile of the bitterest irony was the only manner in which he expressed his gratitude. His coldness hurt, and his sullenness alarmed her.

Her eyes filled with tears; she motioned to take his hand and press it to her lips; but he drew it back, haughtily and gloomily, and passing her without uttering a word, proceeded to the chamber of Eugene.

But no comfort awaited him there. He found the wretched youth tortured by one of his most violent paroxysms. He raved incessantly of his mother and of the murdered Joscelyn; of the lovely cruel Blanche, and the happy hated Osbright. Every word which fell from his lips either tore open a scarcely healed wound in his father's bosom or inflicted upon it a new one. Rudiger listened with horror and remorse to the recapitulation of the poor Agatha's injuries and sufferings; the mention of Joscelyn's murder re-kindled in his heart the flames of vengeance against Gustavus; but when he collected from Eugene's ravings that the child of that very Gustavus was likely to become his daughter-in-law; that she, whose fatal beauty had robbed his darling son of his reason, and almost of his life, had also fascinated the affections of his heir; and that the proud name of Frankheim was destined to be perpetuated through a descendant of the detested race of Orrenberg; no sooner was this discovery made to him, than his surprise, his alarm, his indignation were extreme, extravagant, ungovernable. He rushed from Eugene's apartment, hastened to that of Magdalena, and entering abruptly, assailed her at once with such a storm of passion, of threats, of vows of vengeance against Blanche, against Osbright, against herself if he should find her privy to her son's attachment, that it was long before the Countess could discover the origin of his frantic behavior.

But when she did discover it, she found all efforts to appease his fury totally unavailing. On the contrary, the attempt to soothe him, and the bare suggestion of the advantages likely to result from Osbright's attachment only served to increase his passion; and after loading his wife with the bitterest reproaches, he was rushing from the chamber, when his eye rested on a letter, which in her agitation had fallen from her bosom unobserved. At the same moment with her lord, she also had perceived the paper; with a cry of terror she hastily caught it from the ground; but Rudiger had recognized his son's handwriting, and Magdalena's evident alarm convincing him that it contained some mystery and that a mystery of no slight importance, be rudely forced the letter from her. One half, however, remained in the hand of the Countess, and she hastened to conceal its contents from discovery by throwing it into a brazier which was burning on the hearth.

It was Osbright's letter, which Brother Peter had delivered not an hour before. Pale and trembling with passion, Rudiger read the avowal of his son's love for Blanche expressed in the most glowing terms, his urgent entreaties that Magdalena would prevail on his father to consent to their union, and his confession that for several days he had remained in concealment at the cell of Brother Peter. He also mentioned that he was to have an interview with Blanche that evening...—and here the letter broke off. The object of that interview, the place of rendezvous, the precise time of meeting, these points were contained in the burned half of the letter; and on these points the alarmed Magdalena resolutely refused to give any information. Threats and entreaties were employed in vain; and having placed guards at her chamber door, lest she should make Osbright aware that his incensed father was apprised of the intended meeting, Rudiger left her to meditate on the most certain means of getting the defenseless Blanche into his power.

Wilfred was summoned to his counsels; but the seneschal refused his assistance, till assured that his lord's designs aimed at the liberty, but not at the life of Blanche; though perhaps had he reasoned justly, he would have known that with a man like Rudiger, whose passions were so impetuous, and who was ever swayed by the impulse of the moment, her liberty once lost, her life could not for one instant be secure. However, at present Rudiger's object was, by getting Blanche into his hands, to prevent the possibility of her marriage with Osbright, and to inflict the bitterest agony on Gustavus by making him tremble with every minute for the life of his darling daughter. He also fancied that her presence might be of great efficacy in restoring Eugene to his senses; but he swore with dreadful imprecations that if she failed to produce that beneficial effect, she should be the lunatic's only nurse and continual attendant and should pass the remainder of her existence in witnessing the frantic transports of the wretch whom her fatal charms had ruined. Such being his avowed objects, Wilfred made no longer any scruple of giving his advice. It was accordingly agreed that St. John's Chapel should be watched; that Osbright should be followed to the place of rendezvous; and that Rudiger should hasten thither with a small body of chosen men to seize and convey Blanche to the castle of Frankheim. But Wilfred (who dreaded the resentment of his young lord, should he be known to have had any hand in this business, and in whose power he should be left entirely after Rudiger's decease) stipulated that every possible means should be used to surprise the lady, either previous to her meeting with Osbright or after she had parted from him, but not when the lovers were together.

By taking this precaution, he trusted that Osbright would be kept in ignorance of the persons by whom his mistress had been carried off; all resistance on his part would also be precluded, which otherwise was likely to be very desperate and dangerous to the assailants; and it might even be possible to conceal from him that the scene of his mistress' captivity was the castle of his own father.

To these stipulations Rudiger readily consented; and everything being now arranged, he waited with the utmost impatience for the information that Osbright had set forward from the Chapel of St. John.

CHAPTER XI

"Why does she stop, and look often around.
As she glides down the secret stair;
And why does she pat the shaggy bloodhound.
As he rouses him up from his lair;
And though she passes the postern alone.
Why is not the watchman's bugle blown?"
W. Scott's "Lay of the Last Minstrel."

The time was arrived at which Osbright had engaged to meet Barbara near the drawbridge; but some suspicious circumstances had alarmed Brother Peter and made him intimate to his guest that spies were certainly watching near the chapel gate. There was no other outlet. Osbright, however unwillingly, thought it advisable to protract his departure for a short time; after which Brother Peter was sent out to examine whether the persons whose appearance had excited his suspicions were still loitering near the place. The old man soon returned with the report that all seemed quiet and that in his belief his guest might now set forward without danger of a discovery. But as much time had been lost by this hesitation, the youth doubted not that Blanche and her companion must have long since quitted the castle of Orrenberg and probably had already sheltered themselves within the cave.

Thither he therefore hastened with all possible expedition, and found his conjectures verified.

Blanche and Barbara were safe within St. Hildegarde's Grotto and extremely uneasy at his not arriving. In two hours the drawbridge of Orrenberg Castle would be raised, and Blanche's return prevented; while on the other hand Barbara was uneasy at being so long absent from her decrepit grandmother, and yet could not think of leaving Blanche in the cavern without a companion. The arrival of Osbright at once dispelled their uneasiness. Blanche received him with mingled joy and sorrow; and Barbara, having congratulated the lovers on their meeting, stated her own presence to be now superfluous and entreated permission to return to her grandmother, who (she was certain) must be extremely uneasy at her absence. The permission was readily granted, and she lost no time in profiting by it.

And now did Osbright employ every resource of his eloquence to persuade Blanche that the hour was come when they must either part forever or must part no more. Blanche heard the assurance with agony; but the proposal of flight, of marriage unauthorized by her parents, was rejected by her, not merely with firmness, but even with abhorrence. She owned that to see Osbright no more was the bitterest of all earthly misfortunes, except to live under the consciousness of having merited paternal displeasure. She said that in truth her parting with him would break her heart, but her flight with him would break the hearts of her parents; and she prayed that the vengeance of offended Heaven might fall heavy on her head if she ever planted a single painful feeling in those bosoms, which from the first moment of her birth had only palpitated with love and with anxiety for her.

In answer to this, Osbright said everything that despairing passion could suggest. In vain did Blanche assure him that no persuasion could induce her to act in contradiction to her sense of duty. The youth persisted in pointing out all the advantages likely to result from so slight and so temporary a deviation from the path of strict propriety; and he was still urging his hopeless suit, when a stone fell through the chasm in the grotto's roof, which was at some little distance from the rocky bank on which the lovers were seated. Osbright turned round; a second stone fell, and was followed by a third, accompanied by a low murmuring noise. He listened and fancied that he could distinguish his own name. He rose, and advanced to the chasm.

"Is any one above?" said he aloud; "did any one call" "Hush! hush! sir knight!" interrupted a voice, still whispering. "Speak softly for Heaven's sake; I am Barbara! Oh! Sir knight, I fear that we are all undone, or at least that the Lady Blanche has got into the saddest hole that ever poor lady put her head into. Would you think it, sir knight? I had scarcely set my foot on the outside of the narrow passage... I was going along gaily, singing to myself, and (the Lord knows) thinking of no harm... all on a sudden—'Seize her,' cries a voice like thunder, and in an instant I found myself surrounded by armed men. I fell on my knees, and begged for my life, and with good reason; for one tall terrible knight had got his dagger drawn as if ready to stab me, only his companion caught him by the arm, and bade him remember his oath. 'Right,' said the fierce-one, 'then away with her to the castle! Confine her in the dungeons of the south tower!'—When I heard the word 'dungeon,' I thought, that I should have died outright; so I fell to crying and entreating more than ever, and as luck would have it, the moon just then happened to come from behind a doud. 'Ha!' cried the quiet one, as soon as he saw my face, 'this cannot be the Lady Blanche?' 'Oh! no, no, no!' said I, before I gave myself time to think; 'I am not the Lady Blanche indeed. She is yonder in the cave with Sir Osbright, disguised in boy's clothes, and..."

"You told them so? Imprudent girl! You have undone us all!"

"Alas the day! Sir knight! I was in such a flutter that I scarcely knew what I did or what I said; but as soon as they knew who I really was, they released me and bade me go my ways. I would fain have returned to tell you what had happened; but they would not suffer me, and I was obliged to set forward as if going to my own home. Yet I could not bear to leave you in ignorance of their evil designs; so after a little while I stole back again without noise, and by help of the shrubs and bushes I crept behind the two who appeared to be the chief of the party, so that I could overhear their whole design."

"And that design is... ."—"To seize the Lady Blanche on her leaving the grotto and convey her to the castle of Frankheim, where she is to be shut up in a dungeon, till she consents to marry some young madman who (it seems) has lost his wits for love of her. The fierce one was for going to the grotto and dragging her away this moment; but his companion reminded him of his promise of seizing hei if possible after she had parted with Sir Osbright. 'But suppose,' says the fierce one, 'he should not part with her till she is safe within the walls of Orrenberg?' At last it was agreed between them that they should still wait an hour to see whether Blanche would come out alone; but if that time should elapse without your quitting the cave, sir knight, then the fierce one swore with a thousand dreadful oaths that he would tear her from you with his own hands—'And if he resists,' continued he in a dreadful voice, and he clenched his hands, and I could hear him gnash his teeth, 'if he resists, I will either plunge my sword in the hated girl's heart, or he shall bury his in his father's."

"Your father, Osbright? Your dreadful father?" exclaimed Blanche, wringing her hands. "Now you see, in what danger even this trifling breach of duty has involved me! Oh! My parents, my dear, good parents! How severely am I punished for having clandestinely left for one hour the shelter of your protecting arms!"

"No! no!" said Barbara eagerly, while Osbright vainly endeavored to calm the terrors of his mistress, though his own alarm was scarcely less, "all is not lost yet, dear lady; calm yourself, and listen to me; for as soon as I knew the designs of these villains, I bethought me of a means to save you, and it was for this purpose, that I hazarded to climb the rock and steal hither unobserved to give you this intelligence. It seems that Sir Osbright is in no danger; they will let him pass forth without hindrance, and will rejoice in getting rid of him, in order that they may bear you away to their horrible dungeons without resistance. Now mark what you must do; throw off that long cloak in which Dame Margaret wrapped you up so carefully; array yourself instead in Sir Osbright's armor, and then march forth with a stout heart, his shield on your arm, and his helmet on your head. The shadows of night will doubtless prevent the strangers from observing any difference in your height; the clattering of the armor will confirm them in their mistake; and though to be sure the moon shines brightly just at present, that is a circumstance in your favor; for I heard one of the villains tell the other, that though you were in boy's clothes, there could be no mistaking you for Sir Osbright, who would be known by the device of his shield, and by the scarlet and white plumes on his helmet.

Come, come, make haste, lady; for I warrant you, there is but little time to spare."

Osbright had already divested himself of his breastplate and his glittering casque, and he now hastened to adorn with them the delicate form of Blanche. Confused and terrified in the extreme, she yielded to his entreaties, but frequently compelled both him and Barbara to repeat their assurances that he ran no danger in remaining in the grotto. At length her disguise was complete, and with a beating heart and trembling limbs, she set forward on her dangerous expedition.

No sooner had the lady left the cave than Barbara resumed her discourse. "And now, sir knight," said she, "it will be necessary for you also to play a part. I warrant you, the lady will be no sooner out of hearing than the strangers will hurry hither to secure their prize; and should they discover her flight immediately, they may still be in time to prevent her escape. Therefore wrap yourself up in her scarlet mantle, and conceal your face under the large slouched hat which she has left behind her; they are aware that she is in male apparel, and by disguising your voice a little, you may easily persuade them that you are the person whom they seek till she is safe at Orrenberg. That's right! Now then the hat!—Hark! I hear the noise of armor. Keep up the deception as long as you can; you know, they can but carry you to your own castle; and as it seems that the chief of these strangers is your own father, at worst you have only to discover... they are here! Hush!"

Barbara was correct. Count Rudiger and his attendants had suffered the trembling Blanche to pass unmolested through their ambuscade; they only marked the clank of her arms and the waving of her parti-colored plumes; while the faintness of her step, and that she tottered under the weight of the ponderous shield, passed entirely unobserved. Yet as she drew near the outlet of the rocky path, she once heard a voice whisper from among some bushes—"Now then! Now!"—and the sound appeared to her the sentence of death. Her pulse ceased to beat; she staggered, and caught at a projection of the rock; but presently another voice whispered eagerly in reply—"No!

No! Be silent, fool! 'Tis Sir Osbright! I know him by that casque" ;— and she felt her hopes and her spirits revive. She rushed forward with renewed vigor, and in a few minutes found herself in the great road leading to Orrenberg.

"Now praised be the Virgin!" she exclaimed in a rapture of gratitude, "I am safe!"—when at that moment she found herself seized with violence; her lance was wrested from her hand, and on looking round she perceived herself surrounded by armed men. A shout of exultation immediately followed her capture.

"What is the matter?" exclaimed a warrior, at whose approach the crowd gave way, and in whose voice Blanche recognized with shame and terror the voice of her father. But the visor of her casque was closed, and he little guessed that the warrior who stood before him was the daughter whom he believed secure in the castle of Orrenberg.."The business is half done, my lord!" was the answer. "I should know that helmet and shield among a thousand; and I here present you (without the capture costing you a single blow) with that redoubtable warrior, Osbright of Frankheim."

"Sir Osbright?" cried Gustavus. "Maurice, are you certain of what you assert?—Nay then, this is indeed a prize! But time permits not... . Fear nothing, sir knight; your treatment shall be noble, but for the present you must remain my prisoner. Let six of you convey him to the castle, and confine him in the state-chamber, adjoining to the great hail. Guard him honorably, but closely, and see that no one has access to him. Now then for Rudiger! Away!" Gustavus said, and hastened toward the grotto; and now Blanche found herself compelled to visit the castle of her parents, as an enemy and a captive. However, her plan was already arranged. She determined to keep her secret till safe within the walls of Orrenberg. Once arrived there, she meant to request an interview with her mother, confess to her the whole of her imprudence, and entreat her assistance in repairing it. She doubted not that the strength of maternal tenderness would soon conquer the first emotions of resentment; that Ulrica would find some means of enabling her to regain her own chamber undiscovered; and that as the disappearance of the

104

supposed Osbright might easily be accounted for by his having effected his escape by bribing his guards, or any other artifice, her fault and her danger on this adventurous night might effectually be kept from the knowledge of her father. Such were the designs of Blanche; and having thus arranged them to her satisfaction, she prosecuted her journey to Orrenberg with a less heavy heart.

CHAPTER XII

—"Even-handed Justice
Commends the ingredients of the poisoned chalice
To our own lips."—
Macbeth.

A domestic, whom Count Rudiger had chastised for some trivial fault with unjustifiable severity, in revenge had fled to the castle of Orrenberg and informed its lord that both Osbright and his father were in St. Hildegarde's Grotto, slightly attended, and might easily be surprised. Gustavus failed not to employ so fortunate and unhoped-for an opportunity of getting his chief enemies into his power. He immediately set forward with all the forces which he could muster—and so great was the superiority of his numbers, that in spite of Rudiger's resistance (who exposed his life on this occasion with all the inconsiderate fury of a madman and performed prodigies of valor almost incredible) the small body of Frankheimers were soon put to flight, and their chief was conveyed a prisoner to the castle of Orrenberg.

Now then it was in the power of Gustavus to take a full revenge on his furious kinsman and secure to himself, by the deaths of Rudiger and his son, the entire possessions of the haughty house of Frankheim; but to profit by this opportunity was not in the noble and forgiving nature of Gustavus; he meditated a more honorable vengeance. His own injuries were already forgotten; the death of Ottokar was still remembered, but remembered with grief, not rage. His enemies were totally in his power; that consideration was sufficient to make him view them no longer as enemies; and he seized with eagerness this opportunity of evincing the disinterestedness of his wishes and the sincerity of his professions of good will by a proof so dear and striking as should effectually banish all future mistrust, even from the suspicious bosom of Rudiger. He communicated his intentions to Sir Lennard, who on that evening had arrived with his promised succors at Orrenberg. The worthy knight sanctioned the plan with his warmest approbation, and

Gustavus now hastened, with a heart glowing with delight at the thought of doing a great and generous act, to explain himself to his indignant prisoner.

The great hall was the scene of this interview between the hostile kinsmen. His guards had caused Rudiger's wounds to be carefully dressed, but had thought it proper to restrain him by chains from committing acts of violence. Gustavus, however, no sooner observed this precaution, than he ordered the fetters to be removed; but the sullen captive neither thanked the servants for their care of his wounds nor the master for the restoration of his liberty. He looked on all around him with an air of haughty indifference; but while he listened to Gustavus's professions of good will and proposals for a mutual oblivion of past injuries, the expression of gratified malice glared terribly in his burning eyeballs.

"In short," said Gustavus in conclusion, "I am convinced that the numerous causes which have occasioned the mutual alienation of our hearts and families arose entirely from misinterpretation of accidental circumstances, and not from any Intention of offense, or desire to inflict a premeditated injury. Your suspicions are easily excited; those of my wife are not more difficult to rouse; every trifle was exaggerated, every fact was misrepresented, and suppositions were counted as facts. It is my most earnest wish to root out all misunderstanding forever, and I know of no more certain means than a union of our children, the union of Osbright and Blanche."

"Blanche?" repeated Rudiger "Blanche? Nay, 'tis a most fortunate idea! I only doubt the facility of..."

"Nothing can be effected more easily!" interrupted Gustavus, rejoiced to find his proposal so favorably received. "They love each other... have loved each other long, and..."

"True! I have heard so! Osbright loves your daughter fondly; and no doubt you love her fondly, too?"

"Fondly? Passionately! She is the joy of my existence, the being on whom alone I depend for the whole happiness of my future life!"

"Indeed? That is still better—I rejoice to hear it—there is a youth at home... His name is Eugene... He too loves her passionately... madly, indeed, I might say... But she, you think, loves Osbright?"

"Think it? I know it! It was but this morning that she assured me so ardently that her heart burned for him with such true affection..."

"Nay, it may be so; you must know best; and yet I cannot help suspecting, that her heart feels colder toward him now than it did this morning."

"Your suspicions are unjust, Count Rudiger. Blanche is no capricious... But you shall hear her own lips declare her sentiments. She shall be called hither instantly, and..."

"By no means," cried Rudiger hastily, while he detained his host. "By no means! She is probably retired to rest; I do not wish her to be disturbed; I do not even wish to see her... till Osbright shall present her to me as his bride."

"That may be done this instant; you are not yet aware, Count Rudiger that you are not the only captive of rank whom this night's adventure has thrown into my power. Your son inhabits yonder chamber."

Instantly the expression of Rudiger's countenance changed. He turned pale, and starting from his chair grasped the arm of his seneschal, who had been captured with him in the cave and had accompanied him to Orrenberg.

"My son here?" he exclaimed. "Here! in your power!"

A similar dismay seemed to have taken possession of the seneschal.."I warned you," he replied in broken accents; "I told you... I charged you..."

"Peace, babbler!" interrupted his lord passionately; while Gustavus thus resumed his discourse.

"Yes; Osbright, on leaving the cave, was seized by my followers, and conveyed hither; but calm this agitation, Count, which doubtless is caused by your unjust suspicions respecting the death of your younger son. Your elder, your only one, is now in my hands, and with a single word could I annihilate your whole race. But fear nothing; I would rather perish myself than pronounce that word. Osbright's liberty shall prove to you that I am innocent of the death of Joscelyn; he shall be immediately restored to you, and I only ask in return your consent to his union with my sole heiress, with my darling child."

"I consent!" cried Rudiger eagerly. "I consent to that, to everything! Only give me back my son; suffer us to depart this instant, and to-morrow name your own conditions."

"You shall be obeyed," answered Gustavus, and ordered the doors of the captive's chamber to be thrown open, and himself conducted to their presence. "But," he continued, addressing himself to Rudiger, "surely you will not depart immediately. 'Tis late; the espousals may take place to-morrow; a messenger may be dispatched to inform the Lady Magdalena of the cause which detains you; then tarry here this night, and..."

"This night?" exclaimed Rudiger wildly; "no, no! Not an hour! Not an instant! Count of Orrenberg, would you extort my consent to this union? Would you believe this reconciliation to be sincere, if made with your captives? No! Be generous! Give me back my son without conditions; restore us to liberty; then send your herald to the castle of Frankheim tomorrow and receive my answer, free and uncontrolled."

"Be it so!" said Gustavus; and at the same moment the captive knight entered the hall. The Count of Frankheim, in spite of his agitation (which increased with every moment), recognized the well-known shield and helmet; and before Gustavus had time to explain what had happened, he hastily commanded the youth to follow him. But the youth obeyed not the command. Again it was repeated, and still he remained motionless. Rudiger, whose impatience by this time amounted almost to frenzy, rushed forward to grasp his son's hand, and draw him by force from the apartment. The youth started back with a cry of terror, and retreating nearer to the Count of Orrenberg, seemed to implore his protection against his incensed father. Gustavus endeavored to reassure him.

"Fear nothing, noble youth!" said he. "Your father knows your attachment and approves it. We are no longer enemies; your union with my daughter is settled, and you will only leave this castle tonight that you may return to it tomorrow as the acknowledged bridegroom of your Blanche."

"Indeed?" exclaimed the young knight in joyful surprise. "Oh! Happy tidings! Now then I need nothing more to complete my happiness... nothing but my father's pardon—then pardon me, my father," he continued, at the same time throwing off his ponderous casque, and falling at the feet of Gustavus. "Oh! Pardon your penitent, your imprudent child!"

"Amazement!" exclaimed the Count of Orrenberg. "'Tis Blanche!"

"Blanche?" cried Rudiger, "Blanche in Osbright's armor? Oh! Wilfred, Wilfred! Whom then...? Speak, girl, speak! Explain... oh! Lose not a moment... you know not the fears the agonies... speak, oh! Speak!"

Agitated by hope, blushing at her imprudence, confused by the rapidity and violence with which Rudiger questioned her, it was with difficulty that Blanche related the adventures of the cave to her astonished auditors; but Rudiger soon heard enough to guess the rest. He understood that the lovers had been aware of his approach; that they had changed habits; that disguised as Blanche, Osbright had remained in the cavern; he required to know no more! A shriek of horror interrupted the narrative; his countenance expressed all the agonies of despair; he seemed to be some fiend rather than a human being.

"The blow is struck!" he exclaimed; "'tis past! All is over!—Agony!—Madness!—Yet 'tis possible... To the cave! To the cave! To save him, or to die!" he said, and rushed out of the hall.

"Oh! follow him!" cried Wilfred, wringing his hands; "drag him from the cavern! Nay, nay! Detain me not! His brain will turn... his heart will break... He promised so solemnly... but his violence ... . his passions ... a sudden burst of fury... let me be gone! For the love of Heaven, oh! Let me depart this moment."

And breaking from Gustavus, who wished him to explain the cause of this excessive agitation, the seneschal followed his master, who had already crossed the drawbridge with the rapidity of an eagle.

After a few words to tranquilize his affrighted daughter, the Count of Orrenberg judged it best to pursue the fugitives and learn the cause of their alarm; but before he could leave the hall, a fresh incident obstructed his progress. A young girl, bathed in tears, pale as a specter, and her garments spotted with blood, rushed wildly into the room, and threw herself sobbing at the feet of Blanche. It was Barbara.

"He is gone!" she exclaimed, wringing her hands. "Oh! Lady, lady; he is gone! From the rock above I heard the clank of the assassin's armor as he rushed into the cavern. 'Blanche! Blanche!' he cried; 'Blanche of Orrenberg!' 'Here I am!' answered the poor victim, 'what would you with Blanche?' 'Ha! sorceress!' cried again the terrible voice; 'take this! 'Tis Eugene who sends it you!'—and then... oh! then I saw the weapon gleam... I heard a dreadful shriek... I heard no more!—I lost my senses. When they returned, all was hushed—I ventured down from the rock... I stole into the cave... I dragged him into the light... he was bloody... he was cold... he was dead!"

"Whom? Whom?" exclaimed Blanche, almost frantic with alarm.

"Oh! Osbright! Osbright!" answered the sobbing girl; and Blanche fell lifeless at the feet of her father.

At the door of St. Hildegarde's cave stood the wretched Rudiger; before him lay a corpse, on which he gazed for a few moments in silent agony. At length with desperate resolution he drew away the large hat which overshadowed the face of the dead person, and the moonbeams shone full upon his features. Rudiger knew those features well! He tore off the scarlet robe in which the body was enveloped; he saw a large wound on the breast; he saw his own dagger in the wound; he snatched it forth, plunged it in his heart, and then murmuring the name of Osbright, the slave of passion sank upon his victim's body, and sank to rise no more!

Blanche was restored to life, but her happiness was fled forever. She languished through a few mournful years, and then sought the grave, whither her broken-hearted father soon followed his darling. Then fatal inheritance passed into another family, and the proud race of Frankheim closed its illustrious line forever.

At the expiration of some years, Eugene was unhappy enough to recover his senses sufficiently to know that Blanche was already numbered among the dead. He visited her tomb, wept, and prayed there; then fixed the Cross upon his bosom, and wandered in pilgrim's weeds to the Holy Land. He was never heard of more; but with a frame so delicate, intellect so shattered, and a heart so wounded, doubtless his sufferings could not be long.

Magdalena and Ulrica, these sisters in calamity, retired to the convent of St. Hildegarde, where they soon after assumed the veil, and in whose chapel they caused a stately tomb to be erected over the ashes of their departed children. Here every day they met to indulge their common sorrows; here every night they joined in prayer for the eternal happiness of those dear ones; here during many years of unavailing anguish they bathed with tears the marble tablet on which stood engraved these words, so mournful, so fatal, and so true, "Here rest the Victims of Mistrust."

THE END

CPSIA information can be obtained
at www.ICGtesting.com
Printed in the USA
BVHW080757160621
609629BV00003B/324